If You Want To Know What We Are

A Carlos Bulosan Reader

Originally Edited by
E. San Juan, Jr.

With an Introduction by
Leigh Bristol-Kagan

West End Press

This volume owes its existence to E. San Juan, Jr., who edited and compiled the original version of the manuscript. Our thanks also to Leigh Bristol-Kagan, who inspired the project, and Russell Leong, who provided needed encouragement.

For permission to print this material, we wish to thank, as well as Mr. Aurelio Bulosan, the University of Washington Libraries, in which much of the Carlos Bulosan manuscript collection is housed. In addition, we acknowledge publication of these materials, in the following places.

Labor and Capital, *Commonwealth Times*, June 15, 1937.
My Education, *Amerasia Journal*, 1979, Vol. 6, No. 1, 113-19.
——————, in *The Power of the People*, ed. E. San Juan, Jr., Ontario, Canada, 1977.
How My Stories Were Written, *Solidarity*, September, 1971, 28-31.
The Story of a Letter, *New Masses*, April 30, 1946, No. 59, 11-13.
As Long as the Grass Shall Grow, *Common Ground*, Summer 1949, Vol. 9, No. 4, 38-43.
——————, *Sez*, 1983, No. 4 (forthcoming).
Be American, *Amerasia Journal*, 1977, Vol. 4, No. 1, 157-63.
Homecoming, *Amerasia Journal*, 1979, Vol. 6, No. 1, 75-81.
I Would Remember, *Amerasia Journal*, 1979, Vol. 6, No. 1, 95-99.
To My Countrymen, Biography, Hymn to a Man Who Failed, Factory Town, *Amerasia Journal*, 1979, Vol. 6, No. 1, 112, 103, 105, 106.

Cover photo from *Letters in Exile*, UCLA Asian American Studies Center, 1976, with permission.

Table of Contents

Introduction

Carlos Bulosan was born on November 24, 1913 in the town of Binalonan, Pangasinan province, in Luzon, in the central Philippines. He spent his childhood working in the fields with his father and helping his mother sell salted fish in the public market. He attended school when he could, cutting short his education in high school. He left for America in 1930, and landed in Seattle. In the United States, he worked up and down the West Coast, mostly as a migrant worker and union activist, and he became a writer. He wrote about peasant life in the Philippines and Filipino life in America. When he was hospitalized for tuberculosis in 1936, and spent two years in Los Angeles County Hospital, he read voraciously about America and began the decade of his most intensive writing on Filipinos in America. His major work, *America Is in the Heart*, was published in 1946. He continued to write throughout the rest of his life, as his health declined, but published no other major work. He died in Seattle on September 13, 1956.

This volume offers some of Carlos Bulosan's work on the lives and emerging consciousness of Filipinos in America in the 1930s and 1940s. The introduction offers a view of the emergence of Bulosan's consciousness in the same period.

The migration of peasants from the Philippines who became migrant laborers for West Coast agriculture and the Alaskan canneries was concentrated in the 1920s and 1930s, when the Philippines were a U.S. colony. This migration was one in a succession of Asian laborers—who were first brought as a temporary labor force, whose immigration was then terminated on the basis of race by national exclusion laws, and who were finally classified as aliens ineligible for citizenship.

Chinese were brought first. They were excluded in the midst of the depressions of the 1880s and 1890s when their labor power was no longer needed. Japanese took their place in the fields. The success of some of these laborers as farmers became a reason for Japanese exclusion in 1924. The exclusion of the Japanese, at a time when the expansion of fruit and vegetable farms created a new demand for agricultural labor, stimulated the Filipino migration. Filipinos had already been coming to the United States as laborers by 1920, but their numbers increased between 1924 and 1931. Arrivals grew from 5,600 in 1920 to 56,000 in 1931. By that year, a total of 150,000 Filipinos had come to the U.S., and 45,000 of them had returned to the Philippines.

Filipinos picked the crops and moved on, up and down the Pacific coast and to the canneries in Alaska. They were recruited and hired through contractors, at wages frequently lower than those of other migrant workers. With the depression of the 1930s, as white workers became available for migrant labor and as Filipinos struck against the contract system and lowered wages, they too were targeted for exclusion. The social persecution of Filipinos was legalized in the 1930s, when California, Oregon, Nevada and Washington passed laws forbidding marriages between whites and Filipinos. Filipino immigration to the U.S. was arrested by the passage of the Tydings-McDuffie Independence Act in 1934. It provided for the eventual independence of the Philippines, reclassified Filipinos from U.S. nationals to aliens, and then limited their immigration accordingly, to an annual quota of 50 people.

The Filipinos in the 1920s to 1940s still came from a U.S. colony. Their education had taught them that the ideals of democracy, freedom and equality were to be found in America, and had convinced them of the importance of education itself. They came to improve their lives: to work and get an education, and to earn enough money to go home better off than when they came. They were mostly young unmarried men, under the age of 30; there was but one Filipino woman for every 14 Filipino men.

Most Filipinos arrived credulously expecting to be treated as social equals. They found instead that they were wanted only for their labor power. They were placed in the contradictory position of having to work or shift for themselves in the U.S. while their social community was in the Philippines—yet they usually were unable to earn enough to return. Moreover, as subjects of a U.S. colony, they lived in legal limbo. First as U.S. nationals and later as aliens, they were ineligible for U.S. citizenship. Nor were they citizens of their own country. Once in America, they were essentially exiles: They had left the Philippines but they were not part of America. Thus rapidly and violently deprived of realizing their original ideals and goals, Filipinos in America either were victimized by their circumstances or moved to understand and try to change them, individually and collectively.

Carlos Bulosan participated in this historic migration of Filipinos in America. He came expecting to find the ideals of

6

freedom, equality and democracy in America, and to complete his education. He suffered the same disillusionment, dislocation and deprivation as did his countrymen. Arriving at the turning point of the migration, in the 1930s when its contradictions were becoming acute, he worked and was persecuted as were other Filipinos, and he also took part in union organizing.

What began to distinguish him was not only that he educated himself. He also became a writer and in turn made a series of political and literary choices. His ideas apparently coalesced during his illness of 1936-38, when "I had the opportunity to seriously read books which opened all my world of intellectual possibilities—and a grand dream of bettering society for the working man." Reading brought him a systematic explanation of the forces of capitalism operating in America to shatter the lives of Filipinos. But he also decided to make their suffering meaningful so that they might reverse the damage in their lives, and he chose writing to do so. He read widely in the classics of American literature, and was impressed by the democratic character of the writing of Whitman and Melville. But he was in search of literary examples of the collective transcendence of suffering and the recreation of human communities. To this end, he also read Marxist literature. He then turned to Filipinos and eventually to the Philippines for his subjects and his inspiration.

Bulosan thus decided *as a writer* to identify with the Filipinos. He retold their experiences and gave voice to their aspirations. He addressed the Filipinos in his stories, he sided with them in their labor battles, and he refused to distinguish his life from theirs. He thus kept alive his belief in the ideals of freedom, equality and democracy, placed his faith in the realization of these ideals in the hands of the Filipinos, and participated in their struggle as a writer.

A consequence of Bulosan's political and literary choices to identify himself with the Filipinos was that what he said about himself was what he wanted us to know about Filipinos. In various articles and essays, as well as his fiction, he gives conflicting "facts" about himself. His biography as such therefore remains elusive. (It still awaits research and investigation.) For what was important about him, he seems to say, was how he, a Filipino, shared and came to understand the history of his countrymen, and sought a way to transform it by consciously participating in it as a writer.

A further consequence of Bulosan's commitment to the struggle of the Filipinos was that he then faced the question of where and with whom their struggle would be waged and won. Bulosan's writings record and reflect the progression of his answer to this question in the course of his lifetime. Initially, in the 1930s and the first half of the 1940s, he perceived the future as something to be created by Filipino participation in the labor movement of the working class in America. His early stories therefore tended to separate the lives of peasants in the Philippines from those of the Filipino workers in America, or at least to locate the peasant experience of the workers in their past in the Philippines. Over time, especially after the war and with the weakening of the U.S. labor movement, he began to relate the future of Filipinos to that of the peasantry in a national liberation struggle in the Philippines.

The essays in the first section of this volume articulate Bulosan's consciousness as it evolves. They express his initial understanding of capitalism (*Labor and Capital*) and his vocation as a writer (*My Education*), and demonstrate his practice as a writer of stories (*How My Stories Were Written*).

Bulosan's stories reconstruct the lives and consciousness of their subjects. He creates characters or character types and retells their experiences in such a way that their true meaning is revealed. The stories in this volume treat Filipino workers in America, seeking to transform their history *in America*, and also discovering an identity of suffering and a continuity of struggle between themselves and their peasant families *in the Philippines*.

Bulosan's acceptance of his characters is unconditional, as are his affection for and faith in them. It is in fact this love that has permitted the reader to include himself—to see himself—in the characters and to ask himself to learn along with them. For the intimacy with which Bulosan knows his characters makes their vulnerability, his caring for them, and their responsibility for their circumstances equally inescapable.

The process of discovery and involvement is furthered by Bulosan's use of the convention of the storyteller, in the person of the narrator or a character in the story. The object of the storyteller is to make sense of the experiences of the characters, by pointing to the correct conclusions to be drawn from them. Since this object is as important as the characters and experiences them-selves, the reader's attention is brought to discerning the meaning in otherwise chaotic and familiar events.

Bulosan's aim in his stories was thus to empower his subjects (and hence his readers) by teaching them to find the meaning in their suffering and struggle. This approach required not only an active audience: It also required an ongoing struggle, from which to continuously draw inspiration and learn. Both Bulosan and the Filipinos, however, acted within historical circumstances that limited the forms of their struggles. Bulosan's stories therefore could not go much beyond where the experiences of the Filipinos had taken them at the time.

Bulosan's poems, by contrast, are visionary in their very nature. They crystallize his vision of Filipinos united with the working class in a future transformed by their common struggle. The poems in this volume represent some of the facets of this vision. For the Filipinos, he wanted "to create a home...to stake a claim... to change the course of history," so that in the heart of the cities of the industrial world, the pain of their past and of their parents would not have been in vain. For the working class, he wanted to expose and overcome the deprivation of their humanity. Finally, he envisioned a new human undertaking, based on the unity and equality of all workers, in which they gained their freedom by repossessing their labor and their land.

Carlos Bulosan was recognized as a writer in his lifetime both in the United States and in the Philippines. His early poetry found favor in the prestigious poetry magazines of the 1930s. His stories about the Philippines received attention during a period of wartime curiosity about the Islands. They appeared in the early 1940s in such magazines as *The New Yorker* and *Town and Country*, and as a collection, *The Laughter of My Father*, by Harcourt Brace in 1944. As a writer in the war against fascism, he published an elegaic poem, *Voice of Bataan*, in 1943, and placed individual political poems in both left and mainstream journals in the war years. *America Is in the Heart* was brought out in 1946 by Harcourt Brace and widely acclaimed.

In the Philippines, his poem "If You Want To Know What We Are" was included in an anthology published by the Philippine Writers' League in Manila in 1940. It and one of his stories, "My Father's Tragedy," were published in a 1951 volume of Philippine Prose and Poetry for public school students.

The reception of his work thus tended to depend on the interest it held for different audiences at different times.

Shortly after his death, Carlos Bulosan's papers were collected by his friends and deposited at the University of Washington, Seattle, in 1959. A selection of his letters, entitled *Sound of Falling Light: Letters in Exile,* was edited by Dolores Feria and published in Manila in 1960. It was described as a "definitive portrait" of Bulosan as a Filipino intellectual and artist.

The significance of Bulosan and his work became subject to re-interpretation with his rediscovery in the late 1960s and early 1970s. The emergence of Third World activism and consciousness in the U.S. sparked a new interest in Bulosan. The republication of *America Is in the Heart* in paperback in 1973 was an act of reclamation of Asian American history and literature: It has been widely excerpted since, in both historical and literary anthologies. During the same time, the new political and literary context in the Philippines moved discussion of Bulosan's writings beyond that of evaluating his originality as an individual artist. Students explored his originality in his technique of creating a liberating understanding for his subjects of their oppression and struggle. E. San Juan, Jr. published a pioneer interpretation, *Carlos Bulosan and the Imagination of the Class Struggle,* in Quezon City in 1972. Arguing that Bulosan was a revolutionary writer consciously using his art in the struggle against imperialist oppression, San Juan went so far as to unite in his analysis Bulosan's early stories about peasants in the Philippines and his later ones about Filipino workers in America. Under his editorship, a novel about national liberation struggle in the Philippines, *The Power of the People,* was published in 1977; a collection of folk stories, *The Philippines Is in the Heart,* appeared from Quezon City in 1978; and an anthology of selected works on Filipinos in America and the Philippines was published as a special issue of *Amerasia Journal* (vol. 6, no. 1) in 1979. They chart the course of Bulosan's perception, reached in the later 1940s, that the struggle of the Filipinos was linked indissolubly with that of the Philippines.

Bulosan wrote to transform the history of the Filipinos. His aim was to empower them to learn from their experiences. While he did not live to see this transformation completed, he did contribute to the articulation of its consciousness. And today still, he engages us in an understanding not merely of what it was like to be a Filipino, but also of what might be needed to change the course of our own history.

Leigh Bristol-Kagan

Leigh Bristol-Kagan is a scholar of Asian American history. She currently lives and works in St. Paul, Minnesota.

Labor and Capital: *The Coming Catastrophe*

Labor is the issue of the day. It has always been the issue. It is high time we should understand why thousands of workers' lives are sacrificed; why millions of dollars' worth of property are destroyed in the name of labor.

As in all industrial countries, America's wealth is concentrated in the hands of the few. This wealth is socially produced and privately appropriated. This precisely means that the wealth of the United States is produced by the people, the workers as a whole, and distributed by the industrialists. The contradictions of the social production and the private distribution of wealth [brings about] all social problems.

Industrialists are fattened by profits. Profits are sucked from the very blood of the workers. This profiteering scheme is made possible by speed-ups, long hours and brutal methods. It is by driving workers into a most intolerable condition that the profiteers grow impregnable. There is a better term for this condition: barbarism. But do not think they spend their profits in philanthropic ventures. They invest it in the forces of production, machines, etc. They spend it in idle luxury. Have you seen a banker's daughter throwing away thousands of dollars for a sick dog? They pay more attention to animals than to us. Have you seen a manufacturer's machinery housed and guarded by a cordon of armed men? We are nearly [destroyed] in their riot for profits.

But the industrialists have also a quarrel among themselves. The bigger ones pool together and drive out the smaller ones. This struggle goes on until only one or two are left to dictate in the market. The bigger the combines they have, the more enormous profits they acquire, which means more exploitation. This goes on until society constricts and workers are thrown into the streets to starve. Do not believe that economic depressions are natural phenonema. All depressions are made, and inevitable when the markets are overflowing with surplus: Crisis is bound to come. The only solution that capitalism could give is war. This is why the coming war is more threatening and dangerous than the previous ones. All wars are fought for profit. That is why we must sacrifice everything for the prevention of war. For war is not only the slaughter of humanity but also the destruction of culture, the barbarization of man. We must die for peace and not for profit.

Labor and capital are sharp enemies. There never was any amnesty between them and there shall never be. One or the other stay[s]. The most disastrous proposal is compromise between them. This will never do: it only means the demoralization of the workers, the betrayal of these advanced groups working among the exploited and oppressed.

Unionism is one way of fighting for a better living condition. We are lucky to have in this country a considerable strong group which is fighting for us workers. But this is only a stepping-stone available in democracies. Unionism is a way to economic freedom. But we must have political freedom also. We could have this through unionisms. We must have everything or nothing.

My Education

I came to America sixteen years ago from the village where I was born in the Philippines. In reality it was only the beginning of a tortuous search for roots in a new world. I hated absentee-landlordism, not only because it had driven my family from our home and scattered us, but also because it had shattered the life and future of my generation. This system had originated in Spanish times when most of the arable lands and navigable waters were controlled by the church and powerful men in the government. It came down our history, and threatened the security of the peasantry till it became a blight in our national life.

But now that I was in America I felt a vague desire to see what I had not seen in my country. I did not know how I would approach America. I only knew that there must be a common denominator which every immigrant or native American should look for in order to understand her, and be of service to her people. I felt like Columbus embarking upon a long and treacherous voyage. I felt like Icarus escaping from prison to freedom. I did not know that I was coming closer to American *reality*.

I worked for three months in an apple orchard in Sunnyside, in the state of Washington. The labor movement was under persecution and the minorities became the national scapegoat. Toward the end I was disappointed. I had worked on a farm all my life in the Philippines, and now I was working on a farm again. I could not compromise my picture of America with the filthy bunkhouses in which we lived and the falling wooden houses in which the natives lived. This was not the America I wanted to see, but it was the first great lesson in my life.

I moved to another town and found work on a farm again. Then again I moved to another farm town. I followed the crops and the seasons, from Washington to Oregon to California, until I had worked in every town on the Pacific Coast. In the end I was sick with despair. Wherever I went I found the same horror, the same anguish and fear.

I began to ask if this was the real America—and if it was, why did I come? I was sad and confused. But I believed in the other men before me who came and stayed to discover America. I knew they came because there was something in America which needed them and which they needed. Yet slowly I began to doubt the *promise* that was America.

If it took me almost a decade to dispel this doubt, it was because it took me that long to catch a glimpse of the *real* America. The nebulous and dynamic qualities of the dream took hold of me immensely. It became the periscope of my search for roots in America. I was driven back to history. But going back to history was actually a return to the early beginnings of America.

I had picked hops with some Indians under the towering shadow of Mt. Rainier. I had pruned apples with the dispossessed Americans in the rich deltas of the Columbia River. I had cut and packed asparagus in California. I had weeded peas with Japanese in Arizona. I had picked tomatoes with Negroes in Utah. Yet I felt that I did not belong to America. My departure from the Philippines was actually the breaking of my ground, the tearing up of my roots. As I stayed longer and searched farther, this feeling of not belonging became more acute, until it distorted my early vision of America. I did not know what part of America was mine, and my awareness of not belonging made me desperate and terribly lonely.

The next two years were like a nightmare. There were sixteen million unemployed. I joined those disinherited Americans. Again I saw the rich fields and wide flat lands. I saw them from the top of a passing freight train. Sometimes I saw them from the back of a truck. I became more confused and rootless.

I was sick with despair. I was paralyzed with fear. Everywhere I went I saw the shadow of this country falling. I saw it in the anguish of girls that cried at night. I saw it in the abstract stares of unemployed workers. I saw it in the hollow eyes of children. I saw it in the abuses suffered by immigrants. I saw it in the persecution of the minorities. *I heard some men say that this was America—the dream betrayed. They told me that America was done for—dead. I fought against believing them. Yet, when I was socially strangled, I almost believed what they said about America—that she was dead.*

I do not recall how I actually started to identify myself with America. The men and women around me were just as rootless as I was in those years. I spent the next two years reading in public libraries. How well I remember those long cold nights of winter and the months of unemployment. Perhaps the gambling houses that opened only at night with one free meal for everybody—perhaps reading at the libraries in the daytime and waiting for the dark to hide my dirty clothes in the streets—perhaps all these terrible humiliations gave me the courage to fight through it all, until the months passed into years of hope and the *will* to proceed became obdurate and illumined with a sincere affinity for America. Finally, I realized that the great men who contributed something positive to the growth of America also suffered and were lonely.

I read more books, and became convinced that it was the duty of the artist to trace the origin of the disease that was festering in American life. I was beginning to be aware of the dynamic social ideas that were disturbing the minds of leading artists and writers in America. I felt angry with those who fled away from her. I hated the expatriates in Paris and Madrid. I studied Whitman with naive anticipations, hoping to find in him an affirmation of my growing faith in America. For a while I was inclined to believe that Whitman was the key to my search for roots. And I found that he also was terribly lonely, and he wrote of an America that would be.

I began to wonder about those who stayed in America and suffered the narrowness of the society in which they lived. I read Melville and Poe, who chose to live and work in a narrow world. I became intimate with their humiliations and defeats, their hopes and high moments of success. Then I began to hate the crass materialism of our age and the powerful chains and combines that strangled human life and made the world a horrible place to live in. Slowly, I was beginning to feel that I had found a place in America. The fight to hold on to this feeling convinced me that I was becoming a growing part of living America.

It was now toward the end of 1935, and the trade union movement was in turmoil. The old American Federation of Labor was losing power and a new union was being born. I started to write my own impressions of America. Now I was beginning to give meaning to my life. It was a discovery of America and myself. Being able to write, now, was a personal triumph and a definite identification with a living tradition. I began to recognize the forces that had driven many Americans to other countries and had made those who stayed at home homeless. *Those who went away never escaped from themselves; those who stayed at home never found themselves.*

I determined to find out why the artist took flight or revolted against his heritage. Then it was that, doing organization work among agricultural workers, I fell sick with a disease caused by the years of hunger and congested living. I was forced to lie in a hospital for more than two years. Now, all that I had won seemed irrelevant to my life. Here I was dying—six years after my arrival in America. What was wrong? Was America so dislocated that she had no more place for the immigrant?

I could not believe that the resources of this country were exhausted. I almost died in the hospital. I survived death because I was determined to convince those who had lost faith in America. I knew that in convincing them I would be convincing myself that America was not dead.

The Civil War in Spain was going on, it was another factor that gave coherence to the turmoil and confusion [in] my life. The ruthless bombings of churches and hospitals by German and Italian planes clarified some of my beliefs. I believe that this intellectual and spiritual participation in the Spanish conflict fired in me a new vision of life.

It was at this period that the Congress of Industrial Organizations came to power in industry. At last its militant stand in labor disputes reinvigorated me. Some of my democratic beliefs were confirmed. I felt that I had found the mainsprings of American democracy. In this feeling I found some coherence and direction and the impulse to create became more ardent and necessary.

America's most articulate artists were stirring. They refused to follow the example of those who went into voluntary exile and those who stayed at home and were angry with America. They knew that they could truly work if they stayed near their roots and walked proudly in familiar streets. They no longer created alone. They framed a program broad enough to cover the different aspects of their needs and abilities. It was not a vow to write for art's sake.

I found a new release. I reacted to it as a sensitive artist of my generation without losing my firm belief that America was happy and alive if her artists were happy and alive. But Spain was lost and a grand dream was lost with her. The equilibrium of the world was dislocated, and the writers were greatly affected by the setback of democratic forces.

I tried in the next two years to work with the progressive forces. But some of the organizations dribbled into personal quarrels and selfish motives. There were individuals who were saturated with the false values of capitalism and the insidiousness of their bourgeois prejudices poisoned their whole thinking. I became convinced that they could not liberate America from decay. And I became doubly convinced, as Hitler seized one country after another, that their prejudices must be challenged by a stronger faith in America.

We were now moving toward the end of another decade. Writing was not sufficient. Labor demanded the active collaboration of writers. In the course of eight years I had relived the whole course of American history. I drew inspiration from my active participation in the workers' movement. *The most decisive move that the writer could make was to take his stand with the workers.*

I had a preliminary knowledge of American history to guide me. What could I do? I had read *Gone with the Wind*, and saw the extent of the lie that corrupted the American dream. I read Dreiser, Anderson, Lewis, and their younger contemporaries: Faulkner, Hemingway, Caldwell, Steinbeck. I had hoped to find in these writers a weapon strong enough to blast the walls that imprisoned the American soul. But they were merely describing the disease— they did not reveal any evidence that they knew how to eradicate it.

Hemingway was too preoccupied with himself, and consequently he wrote of himself and his frustrations. I was also disappointed with Faulkner. Why did he give form to decay? And Caldwell, Steinbeck—why did they write in costume? And Odets, why *only* middle class disintegration? Am I not an immigrant like Louis Adamic? Perhaps I could not understand America like Richard Wright, but I felt that I would be ineffectual if I did not return to my own people. I believed that my work would be more vital and useful if I dedicated it to the cause of my own people.

It was now almost ten years since I had landed in America. But as we moved rapidly toward the war with Japan, I realized how foolish it was to believe that I could define roots in terms of places and persons. I knew, then, that I would be as rootless in the Philippines as I was in America, because these roots are not physical things but the quality of faith deeply left and clearly understood and integrated in one's life. The roots I was looking for were not physical but intellectual and spiritual things. In fact, I was looking for a common faith to believe in and of which I could be a growing part.

Now I knew that I was living in the collective era. Where was I to begin? I read Marxist literature. Russia was then much in the minds of the contemporaries. In the Soviet system we seemed to

19

have found a workable system and a common belief that bound races and peoples together for a creative purpose. I studied Russian history as I had studied American history. I tried to explain the incoherence of my life on the ground that I was living in a decaying capitalist society.

Then we felt that something was bound to happen in America. Socialist thinking was spreading among the workers, professionals and intellectuals. Labor demanded immediate political action. For the first time a collective faith seemed to have appeared. To most of us it was a revelation—and a new morning in America. Here was a collective faith dynamic enough to release the creative spirit that was long thwarted in America. My personal predicaments seemed to vanish and for the first time I could feel myself growing and becoming a living part of America.

It was now the middle of 1941. The dark clouds of war were approaching our shores. Then December 7 came to awaken a decadent world. Japan offered us a powerful collective faith that was pervasive enough to sweep away our fears and doubts of America. Suddenly I began to see the dark forces that had uprooted me from my native land, and had driven me to a narrow corner of life in America. At last the full significance of my search for roots came to me, because the war with Japan and against Fascism revealed the whole meaning of the fears that had driven me as a young writer into hunger and disease and despair.

I wrote in my diary: "It is well that we in America take nourishment from a common spring. The Four Freedoms may not be realized in our times but if the war against Fascism ends, we may be sure that we have been motivated by a native force dynamic enough to give form to the creative spirit in America. Now I believe that all of us in America must be bound together by a common faith and work toward our goal...."

How My Stories Were Written

A few years ago, I wrote for the *Writer* a brief article revealing the compelling force that propelled me from an obscure occupation to the rewarding writing of short stories. That *force* was anger born of a rebellious dissatisfaction with everything around me.

When I sold my first story, I was still a laborer at a fish cannery in San Pedro, California. But immediately afterward letters came asking me how I became a writer, pointedly emphasizing the fact that I have a very limited formal education, and why was I writing proficiently in a language which is not my own?

The making of a writer is not by accident. It takes years of painstaking preparation, whether one knows or not that he is on the path of a writing career; of extensive reading of significant contemporary writings and the classics of literature, and of intensive experimental writing, before one is ready to synthesize reading, writing and experience into a solid premise from which one should begin a difficult career as a writer.

But the type of writing which flows from such a premise depends completely on the sensibility of the individual and his ability to crystallize his thoughts; whether he would interpret reality and maintain that art is not alien to life but a transmutation of it in artistic terms, or indifferently deny life and completely escape from it, as though the immediacy of man's problems of existence were not the concern of the writer.

I did not know what kind of a writer I would become. Not having known any writer personally, I had to grope my way in the dark. And what a heartbreaking journey that was! I thought I could write commercial stories for the high-paying slick magazines—and thus I wrote dozens of stories that came back as fast as I sent them out. Then the foolish notion came to me that the literary magazines were my natural field, since the literary story seemed to me the easiest thing to write; so dozens of stories again came back as fast as I sent them out.

Remember that these stories dealt with a life that was unknown to me. I wrote about imagined experiences of body and mind, put words in the mouths of characters that were ridiculously alien to them, it seems to me now. I even carefully plotted: the compulsive beginning, the staggering anti-climax or denouement, and the heartwarming or heartbreaking climax.

You see, I denied myself: my own experiences seemed irrelevant, my own thoughts seemed innocuous, my own perceptions seemed chaotic and ambiguous. These are some of the dilemmas of the beginner.

It was only when I began to write about the life and people I have known that a certain measure of confidence began to form as my periscope for future writing. And as this confidence grew and took a definite shape, I discovered that the actual process of writing was easy—almost as easy as breathing.

I wrote about my family and the village where I had been born. I wrote about my friends and myself in America, placing my characters in localities familiar to me, and always wrapping them up in contemporary events. Except, of course, my stories based on Philippine folk tales and legends. But even these were given a background known to me. And more, I humanized my legendary and folktale characters, so that reading them, it would be impossible to determine which is fact and which is the flight of imagination.

I have written many stories of this type. I will now tell you about the vast storehouse of rich material with which my childhood world endowed me so generously that I can go on indefinitely writing folkwise stories based on the hard core of reality. It is about an old man in my childhood.

It is true there are mountains which are green all the year round bordering the northside of the province of Pangasinan, my own native province, in the island of Luzon. It is true there is a fertile valley under the shadows of these mountains from which the peasants have been scratching a living since the dawn of Philippine history. And these simple peasants, backward still in their ways and understanding of the world, have not yet discarded the primitive tools that their forefathers had used centuries before them, in the beginning of a settlement that was to become the most densely packed population section of the island. The passing of time and the intensification of settlers in this valley helped preserve a common folklore that was related from mouth to mouth and from generation to generation, until it was no longer possible to distinguish which tale was indigenous to the people living there and which one was borrowed from the other tribes and moulded into their own. But the telling of these tales was so enchanting, so uncommonly charming, that no man now questions the truth of their origin and the validity of their existence in times past.

It is also true that there is a village called Namgusmana, where I had been born, in this valley where a wayward river runs uncharted and waters the plains on its journey to the open seas. Here the farmers plant rice when the rains come from the mountains to the north, and corn when the sun shines, and sugarcane when soothing winds blow from the other horizon in the south and sometimes in the west, so that the fields are verdant with vegetation every day of the year.

But it is also true that when the moon was bright in the sky an old man whose age no one could remember because he was born long, long ago, in the era of the great distress of the land, who came down from his mysterious dwelling in the mountains and walked in our village and the children stoned him when he did not tell his tales of long ago: now it is true that he sometimes sat under a mango tree at the edge of the village to relate a story over a cup of red wine or when he was given a handful of boiled rice, and the children would scatter attentively on the grass around him, and the men and women would stand silently further away to catch every word, because there was no telling when he had a new tale about the people who had wandered and lived and died in that valley ages ago.

It happens that it is also true, that I heard this old man tell his tales many a time when I was a little boy. At first he did not notice my presence among the crowd of children that listened to him, but as time went by he began to notice me until at last he concentrated his telling to me.

"I have noticed your attentiveness," he said to me one day. "Do you believe these tales?"

"I believe them, Apo Lacay," I told him.

"But why?" he demanded. "These are merely the tales of an old and forgotten man who has lived beyond his time. There are others who can tell you more fascinating stories of what is happening today."

"There is wisdom in your words, Apo Lacay," I said respectfully. "Besides, I will go away some day and I would like to remember what kind of people lived here a long time past."

"You will go to a land far away," he asked. There was a sudden gleam in his eyes but just as suddenly it vanished, and a deep melancholy spread across his wrinkled face. "But you will never

23

return, never come back to this valley."

I could not answer him then, or the day after, or long afterward—not even when I came to this land far away, remembering him.

"Everybody dies, but no man comes home again," he said sadly. "No man comes to bathe in the cool water of the river, to watch the golden grain in the fields, to know the grandeur of the meadow lark on the wing. No man comes back to feel the green loam of the land with his bare feet, to touch the rich soil with his loving hands, to see the earth move under him as he walks under the silent skies."

"I will come back, Apo Lacay," I said.

He looked at me silently and long, then there were tiny tears in his eyes.

"Son, he said at last, touching my head with his faded hands, "I will go home now."

He reached for his cane and walked away. He did not come again. Many years passed, and everybody thought he was dead. And then that year of my grand awakening, I decided to look for the old man. I went to the mountains and looked for him, sleeping in several forests and crossing many ravines and hills, shouting in the wind and climbing the tallest trees to see some signs of human habitation on the caves that dotted the mountainside. And at last I found him sitting by a small stream.

"Good morning, Apo Lacay," I greeted him.

He stirred but his face was lifted toward the sun.

"I came to say goodbye," I told him.

"So it is you," he said. "I thought you left long ago."

"Now is the time, Apo Lacay," I said. "But tell me this: is it not dangerous to live all by yourself in the mountains?"

"What is there to fear in the night? The beasts, the birds, the trees, the storms and tempests—would you be afraid of them? There is nothing to fear in the night, in the heart of night. But in the daylight among men, there is the greatest fear."

"But why, Apo Lacay?"

"In the savage heart of man there dwells the greatest fear among the living."

"But man has a mind."

"That is the seed of all the fear. The mind of man. The beast in the jungle with his ferocious fangs is less dangerous than man with his cultivated mind. It is the heart that counts. The heart is everything, son."

"Is that why you tell the kind of stories you have told us? To make us laugh?"

"Laughter is the beginning of wisdom."

"There is perhaps a great truth in what you have just said. That is why I came to see you. I will leave our country soon and I would like to remember all your stories."

"But why? In that land where you are going, will the people give you something to eat when you retell them? Will you not be afraid the children will stone you?"

"I don't know, Apo Lacay. But this I know: if the retelling of your stories will give me a little wisdom of the heart, then I shall have come home again."

"You mean it will be your book as well as mine? Your words as well as my words, there in that faraway land, my tales going around to the people? My tales will not be forgotten at last?"

"Yes, Apo Lacay. It will be exactly like that, your book as well as mine."

He was silent for a long time. He made a fire by the stream, sat by it and contemplated deeply. Then it seemed to me, watching him lost in thought, he had become a little boy again living all the tales he had told us about a vanished race, listening to the gorgeous laughter of men in the midst of abject poverty and tyranny. For that was the time of his childhood, in the age of great distress and calamity in the land, when the fury of an invading race impaled their hearts in the tragic cross of slavery and ignorance. And that was why they had all become that way, sick in soul and mind, devoid of humanity, living like beasts in the jungle of their capitivity. But this man who had survived them all, surviving a full century of change and now living in the first murmurs of a twilight and the dawn of reason and progress, was the sole surviving witness of the cruelty and dehumanization of man by another man, but whose tales were taken for laughter and the foolish words of a lonely old man who had lived far beyond his time.

When I looked at him again he was already dead. His passing was so quiet and natural that I did not feel any sadness. I dug a grave by the stream and buried him with the soft murmur of the trees all around me. Then I walked down the mountains and into the valley of home, but which was no longer a home. Sometime afterward I boarded a big boat that took me to this land far away.

And now in America, writing many years later, I do not exactly know which were the words of the old man of the mountains and which are mine. But they are his tales as well as mine, so I hope we have written stories that really belong to everyone in that valley beautiful beyond any telling of it.

Passage into Life

1

Allos was five when he first became aware of the world.

One morning his father sent him to the house of the landlord with a basket of goat meat. He was admitted by a servant who took him into the house. The landlord and his family were having dinner, and when Allos entered the dining room they stopped eating and covered their noses.

"What is in that basket?" asked the landlord.

"Goat meat, sir," Allos said.

"Why did you bring it here?" asked the landlord's wife.

"My father told me to give it to you, Madam," he said.

"Who is your father?" asked the landlord.

"My father works on your land, Your Excellency," Allos said humbly.

"We don't eat goat," shouted the landlord. "Take it away!"

"Peasants! Poor peasants!" sneered one of the landlord's children.

Allos went to the door, weak with shame. He ran out of the yard dragging the basket behind him and shouting to the world that he would never go back to that house again.

2

When Allos was six something happened that definitely changed the course of his life.

He was playing with his dog when he saw Narciso running toward the river. Narciso was his age and a good friend. He stopped playing with the dog and ran after Narciso. He ran swiftly, feeling the earth moving away under him, but every stride he made seemed to push him farther from his friend. When he arrived at the river, Narciso had already jumped naked into the water and was shouting to him.

Allos watched him. Narcisco was going downstream. Allos could not understand what was happening. Pausing momentarily at the edge of the high embankment, Allos called to his friend. But at that same instant Narciso's head disappeared under the water.

And then Allos knew.

That evening, when Narciso's body had been found and laid out in a coffin, Allos went into the house silently to see the face of the dead boy for the last time. Tears appeared in his eyes.

Allos suddenly rushed out of the house and ran into the yard where the bright moonlight was shimmering in the guava trees. It was quiet there and for a while he stood crying under a tree, smelling the fragrance of the guavas in bloom. Now a nightingale started singing somewhere in the orchard, followed by another, and still another until the whole yard seemed full of them. He listened, drying his eyes. And when he saw a nightingale singing above his head he began to smile.

And then Allos forgot his dead friend. He burst into a song and started running happily in the moonlight until the trees became while castles sailing on a huge cloud of music.

3

Allos walked behind his mother in the rain. It was his first time to go to the town market. There was a sack of fresh peanuts on his back. His mother carried a big basket of vegetables on her head.

"Are you really going to buy a new straw hat, Mother?" Allos said.

"Yes, son" his mother said. "And if we sell all the peanuts you are carrying, we will also buy a piece of carabao meat for our family."

Allos walked lightly, dreaming of a new straw hat. The rain stopped when they arrived in the public market. They spread a grass mat on the ground in a corner and put their peanuts and vegetables on it.

But nobody came to their corner. Once a man stopped to cast a glance, then hurriedly walked on to a wineshop. In the late afternoon, when the rain began falling again, Allos and his mother gathered their peanuts and vegetables.

They were the last to leave the public market. And Allos, who realized now that he would not have a straw hat, walked blindly, knowing that this day would never be forgotten as long as he lived.

Oh, Allos, hide in the thorns and thickets of the world!

4

Allos was standing in front of the store when the man came to the door and called to him.

"You like to have one of those candies, son?" he asked.

"Yes, sir," Allos said. He had been standing there for an hour wondering how to get the long red stick of candy. "Yes, sir," he said again.

"Well, son, come inside and mop the floor," said the man.

Allos thought that the man was very nice indeed. Eagerly he swept and mopped and dried the floor of the store. When he had put away all the tools in the closet, the man came out of his office and told Allos to cut the grass in the yard.

Allos found a sickle and a long sharp knife in the kitchen. He bent and knelt, swinging the sickle and the knife. Finally he finished the job. He was standing under a tree and wiping the beads of perspiration off his face when the man came out and told him to haul drinking water from the well.

Allos took the large bucket from the rack on the wall and went to the well. He filled all the drinking jars and cans in the store.

"Good boy," said the man. "Now you can have your stick of candy."

The man found a mouldy candy in a corner of the display case and handed it to the boy. Allos grabbed the candy and ran out. But he was so hungry and tired that the candy made him ill. He threw it away and started running toward home.

He had forgotten to thank the man for being so kind and generous.

5

Now, finally, Allos was going to school. On his way home, carrying a big picture book under his arm, he stopped several times in the street and tried to decipher the big words under the pictures. Somewhere in this big book, he thought, was the magic door to all that he wanted to know.

He walked on, thinking of his seven years. At home, if one of his cousins were present, Allos would ask for his help. But when he reached the gate, Allos saw many people hanging on the fence around the house. There was a wild commotion in the yard, and women were crying hysterically and children were bawling loudly.

Allos ran in the yard to see what was going on. He stopped suddenly when he saw that his father was tied to a tree and one of his brothers was beating him with a stick. His uncle was trying to grab away the stick, but his brother's wife was pulling his uncle by the hair. Farther away, under the house, his mother was rolling in the dust with his brother's oldest daughter.

Allos was aroused. A great fury surged in him. He grabbed a piece of wood and rushed upon his cousin, who was already beating his mother's head with all her fury. He drove his cousin away. Then he rushed upon his brother and started beating his legs and arms. He could not reach his head. His brother turned around and kicked him in the stomach. Allos fell in the dust, but for a moment only. Somewhere he saw a big knife, and he grabbed it, running back to his father's rescue.

Now his brother and uncle were grappling like mad dogs in the dust. He went to his father and cut the ropes that bound him. His father suddenly broke loose and rushed upon the two men who were rolling and grunting. Allos jumped upon them with the knife. But several men jumped over the fence and took the knife away from him.

Allos ran across the yard and into the street. He ran furiously for hours until he could not move any more. He sat down weeping. His agony was beyond consolation. When he became aware of his surroundings, night was falling and a few stars were already in the sky. He had wandered far away from home.

Allos walked aimlessly for hours. He stopped to sleep under a tree, but the fear of wild animals made him walk on. He traveled eastward, following the morning star. At last fatigue came upon him, and he lay down beside a stream and went to sleep.

When he woke up the sun was already in the sky. He jumped to his feet, frightened and bewildered. An old farmer was sitting beside him, watching him with amusement.

"Where am I, sir?" Allos asked.

"You are in the village of Batong," said the old man.

"I am far away from home," Allos said.

"And where is that?" asked the old man.

"The village of Togay, sir," he said.

"You are indeed far from home," said the old man. "But you should go home right away. Your parents might be worried about you. Today of all the days of the year is the most significant. Somewhere in this world our Lord, Jesus Christ, is born again. So go home to your parents and rejoice with them."

The old man was so kind, Allos thought. Why was it different at home? But he would go home and ask for forgiveness.

"I don't know how to go home," Allos said finally.

"Well, I have a small cart," said the old man. "It will take you home."

Riding with the old man to his village, Allos knew that he would never forget this man who showed kindness to him.

6

Allos was standing on the corner of his street when he saw several boys stoning a man. He picked up a bamboo stick and ran to the scene.

It was old man Remic. He was covering his head with his hands. One of the older boys hit him on the knee. Remic slowly went down and rolled in the dust.

Allos chased the boys away with his stick. When they were gone he returned to the old man. Remic was already on his feet. He was wiping the blood off his face and legs.

"Thank you, son," Remic told him.

"Why did they stone you, Remic?" Allos asked.

"They think I am crazy," he said. "They think I am all alone in the world."

"You are not crazy, Remic," Allos said. "And you are not alone."

"That is true enough," Remic said. "But they can't understand it. Now it is they who are alone and crazy."

When the old man was gone, Allos picked up the stick again and started running and beating wildly in the wind. He rushed into his yard and grabbed the first tree there and wept silently until his father carried him into the house.

31

7

Night was falling.

Allos took the carabao from its peg and rode homeward. He was the last herdsboy to leave the pasture. The animal was full and lazy, but it was patient and kind to the boy.

Allos washed the carabao in the river. Then the animal walked slowly in the narrow street, its big stomach swaying and thundering like a drum. When they came to the gate, Allos jumped off the carabao's back and toward his house.

It was dark.

Allos, leaning against the carabao, wondered where his people had gone. They were still there when he left for the pasture that morning. He hugged the animal affectionately, not knowing what to do. And for the first time he felt a great need to hear his people shout and laugh and sing again.

Oh, Allos, don't be afraid! The good earth will comfort you in her dark womb!

8

And again the following year, coming home from school, he saw his mother trying to fell a coconut with a long bamboo pole. His mother was short and weak; she gave up after an hour of futile efforts and went back to the house.

Allos found the smallest tree in the yard and climbed it. He was detaching a fruit with one hand and holding tightly on to the trunk with the other when suddenly everything went dark and for a brief moment only he realized that he was falling.

Afterward Allos remembered lying on the ground and the night coming over him. Painfully he rolled over and saw one fruit beside him. Then he knew that he had fallen with it. He crawled toward his house, pushing the coconut slowly with his head. When he came to the ladder, Allos bit the coconut and climbed up step by step. His body was afire and there was a stabbing pain in his head.

Then his mother saw him reaching for the pole on the landing and trying to shove the coconut into the door with his head. His mother shrieked. Allos looked at her for a moment and knew why he had done it, but at the same instant he also ceased to know.

9

Then there was that day when Allos came home and found that all his people were gone. He sat in the kitchen wondering and waiting. When night came he looked into all the pots for something to eat. But they were all empty and clean.

Allos went out of the house and walked to his cousin's house. It was dinner time and his relatives were seated around a small table. There was a steaming boiled chicken and a large platter of pearly white rice on the table. But when his uncle invited him to join them, Allos felt ashamed and forgot his hunger. It was then that he knew how miserable it was to be poor and alone.

Allos went back to his house and boiled some leaves and a handful of grass that he had found in the yard. He ate in the dark knowing that he would never be brave enough to go into the world begging for food or kindness or pity.

10

There was one thing that drove Allos to thinking, and it was watching his mother work all day and half of the night. He knew that his mother woke up at five every morning and started preparing breakfast for the family, and after that, when the members of his family had departed, his mother cleaned the house and washed clothes in the river. At noon, however, she stopped her work and rushed back to the house to prepare lunch, and when this task was performed she returned to the river to finish her washing. Then in the evening, in the midst of the family's laughter, she prepared dinner. When the family was fed, Allos watched his mother clean the dishes and the kitchen. And then, when all the members of the family were in bed except Allos, his mother started ironing the day's washing in the faint lamplight. It was past midnight when he heard his mother creep to her grass mat near the door.

This had been his mother's routine for as long as he could remember. The only variation was when she went to the farm to help his father with the planting and harvesting of rice. Or when she went to the town market to sell a basket of vegetables so that there would be a piece of meat for the family.

Allos often wondered why his mother did not get sick. But one rainy day, carrying a large basket of vegetables, his mother fell under the strain and broke her knee. He helped his mother stumble into the house, running back to the street to pick up the scattered vegetables.

When he returned to the house his mother was writhing with pain. Allos wiped the beads of perspiration off her face, knowing that the world would never again be the same if something fatal happened to his mother.

"I will not believe in God any more if you die, Mother," Allos said.

"Son, little son, you must believe in God always," his mother said.

"Yes, Mother," he said. But Allos knew that he would never believe in God, or in any man, or in himself, if his mother died.

11

Allos was eleven when his older sister came back from the city to live with them. Marcia was a very quiet girl. Allos could not understand it. All the other members of the family were always shouting and laughing and singing. Marcia, however, walked silently in the house and always sat by the window until midnight.

Allos tried to talk to her sometimes, but Marcia only looked at him without saying anything. Her eyes were lifeless when she looked at him.

But one day Allos asked, "Why is my sister Marcia always sitting by the window, Mother?"

"She is waiting for a husband, son," his mother said.

"Is it difficult for her to get a husband?" he asked.

"Yes," his mother answered.

"Why?" Allos wanted to know.

"Because we are poor, son," his mother said finally. "Nobody wants to marry a poor girl."

And Allos, knowing it to be a fact indeed, rushed out of the house wondering why there were poor people. He picked up a stone in the yard and threw it with all his might at a hen that was scratching near the fence. And then he ran furiously down the street crying to himself that when he grew up he would become rich, but when he reached the river he did not know where to get the money.

Allos plunged into the water hoping that he would die. But several farmers came to his rescue and took him home. When his mother asked him why he did it, Allos looked at her with tears in his eyes.

Allos was on his way to church when he saw a big crowd near the wineshop. He rushed to the scene and pushed his way through the crowd of milling men and women. And there in the center was an old man who was bleeding profusely. Several men were beating and kicking him in the face.

Allos was surprised and angry at the same time, because he knew that this old man had been collecting rags and empty bottles for years in his town, but he had never bothered or cheated anyone. He was only an old man who went from house to house buying discarded rags for five centavos per pound and one centavo per empty bottle. He carried a long bamboo pole on his shoulders and at either end hung a basket where he deposited his possessions. The old man usually passed by his house, bent and staggering under his heavy load, and sometimes he stopped near his gate to fan himself with his battered straw hat. He was barefooted and his patched cotton pants were rolled up tightly to his knees, so that Allos could see his spindly legs and knotted veins. That was why Allos was sometimes impelled, when he saw the old man staggering with his load, to go out and offer to help him.

But now the men were beating him and kicking his face in the dust. Allos could not understand it so he fell upon the old man's tormentors and tried to push them away.

A man grabbed him, saying, "Keep out of this, son. What have you got to do with him, anyway?"

"You are hurting him," Allos cried. "He is a very sick old man."

"He is only a Chinaman," said the man.

Allos had never heard the word before. "What is a Chinaman?" he asked.

"A Chinaman is a foreigner in our country and a spreader of foul diseases among our people," the man told him. "This man is a Chinaman."

"I never saw him spread any diseases," Allos protested.

But the man instructed two of the bigger boys to hold Allos, while he went back to the old man and started beating him again. Allos bit and kicked, but in vain. He looked around pleadingly, but no one tried to help the old man. They stood there and watched him rolling in the dust and even emitted cries of joy when he started to bleed. Finally the old man stopped resisting. He lay still near his broken bottles and burning rags.

The crowd began to disperse quickly. And there was Allos, left with the old man in the approaching night. He knelt in the dust and picked up the old man and blew warmly upon his face. And he wondered as he tried to revive the old man's breath what it was that distinguished him from his people.

"He looks the same," Allos murmured. "He even looks like my father." Then he said fearfully, "Wake up, old man. I will tell you we are the same! Please wake up!"

But the old man was already dead.

13

Allos' father was dying. He heard his mother talking with one of his uncles that if they had money his father had a good chance to live. Suddenly he remembered his rich cousin who had just arrived in town with a big car and a beautiful young wife. He rushed out of the house hoping his cousin would be home and willing to help him.

Allos was entering the gate when he saw his cousin coming [out of] the house with his wife. He was royally dressed and there was a shiny black cane in his hand. His wife was dressed beyond imagination. She was smiling widely and looking at the world like a papaya in bloom.

Allos stopped for a moment, wondering how two creatures could be endowed with so much good fortune. And then bravely he rushed toward his cousin, almost colliding into him. But his cousin brushed him away with his cane, away from his immaculate suit and beautiful young wife, and suddenly, Allos felt, away from his only hope and into the dark well of his shame.

His cousin did not even talk to him. When he and his wife were comfortably seated in the car, he opened the window and threw a dime in Allos's direction. And then they drove away.

Allos picked up the small silver dime and looked at it for a long time.

14

Allos was fourteen when he met the stranger. He was wandering aimlessly in a dry river when he saw him. The stranger was lying quietly on the sand. Allos sat beside him.

"Don't be sad, son," said the stranger.

"How did you know I am sad?" Allos asked.

"I know," said the stranger.

Allos did not understand what the stranger meant, but he said, "I have no more father. He died today."

"I'm sorry to hear that, son," said the stranger. "But it is like this with all of us in the world: No one is really an orphan as long as there is another man living. As long as there is one man living and working and thinking on the earth."

"I don't know," Allos said. "I had a very good father. He had worked all his life and when there was not enough to eat in the house he would give up his own portion and offer it to me. I don't know if there is a father like him in the whole world."

"I suppose not," said the stranger. "I had a father, too. And he was a very good father. But he died like your father. Death is not a bad thing. It is only the beginning of a much longer life. It is the beginning of a life that never ends. All your dreams, all the things that you want to do in this world but can't achieve—well, you'll have them all in that other place. And more than that, son. Your father will be waiting for you when you arrive. All your other relatives will be there too, waiting for your homecoming. Yes, that is the home for us all."

"I didn't know that, sir," Allos said finally. "I thought that death is the end of everything."

"You are wrong, son," said the stranger. "Now come with me and I'll show you that you are wrong."

They got up together and crossed the river and walked through a wide valley. They walked on for two days and two nights, stopping now and then to see the land around them. And then on the third day they came to a tall mountain and climbed upward until they reached the top. But it was night again and it was very quiet all around them.

There on the other side of the mountain was an impenetrable darkness, and a silence that had no voice. Allos looked and knew at last that there was a life without end.

He turned to the stranger, saying, "Yes, it is all true..."

Allos watched the stranger walk down the mountain to the other side until he was swallowed by the darkness. He was left alone in the night, but felt that he could contend with whatever would befall him.

He turned back and started to descend toward the valley where he had come from, toward home and his people. When he had crossed the last mountain that divided his land and the unknown country where the stranger had disappeared, Allos stood on the highest peak and watched with a mounting joy the dazzling brilliance of the new sun shining above all his rivers and plains.

Now Allos knew: There in the known world he must go to seek a new life, seek it among the living until he would have enough time to pause and ponder on the mystery of the dead. And so with light steps he walked toward his valley, a song of joy warming his whole being until it became the song of all his living dreams.

The Story of a Letter

When my brother Berto was thirteen he ran away from home and went to Manila. We did not hear from him until eight years later, and he was by that time working in a little town in California. He wrote a letter in English, but we could not read it. Father carried it in his pocket all summer hoping the priest in our village would read it.

The summer ended gloriously and our work on the farm was done. We gathered firewood and cut grass on the hillsides for our animals. The heavy rains came when we were patching the walls of our house. Father and I wore palm raincoats and worked in the mud, rubbing vinegar on our foreheads and throwing it around us to keep the lightning away. The rains ceased suddenly, but the muddy water came down the mountains and flooded the river.

We made a bamboo raft and floated slowly along on the water. Father sat in the center of the raft and took the letter from his pocket. He looked at it for a long time, as though he were committing it to memory. When we reached the village church it was midnight, but there were many people in the yard. We tied our raft to the river bank and dried our clothes on the grass.

A woman came and told us that the priest had died of overeating at a wedding. Father took our clothes off the grass and we put them on. We untied our raft and rowed against the slow currents back to our house. Father was compelled to carry the letter for another year, waiting for the time when my brother Nicasio would come home from school. He was the only one in our family who could read and write.

When the students returned from the cities, Father and I went to town with a sack of fresh peanuts. We stood under the arbor tree in the station and watched every bus that stopped. We heated a pile of dry sand with burning stones and roasted peanuts. At night we sat in the coffee shop and talked to the loafers and gamblers. Then the last student arrived, but my brother Nicasio was not with them. We gave up waiting and went to the village.

When summer came again we plowed the land and planted corn. Then we were informed that my brother Nicasio had gone to America. Father was greatly disappointed. He took the letter from his pocket and locked it in a small box. We put our minds on our work and after two years the letter was forgotten.

Toward the end of my ninth year, a tubercular young man appeared in our village. He wanted to start a school for the children and the men were enthusiastic. The drummer went around the village and announced the good news. The farmers gathered in a vacant lot not far from the cemetery and started building a schoolhouse. They shouted at one another with joy and laughed aloud. The wind carried their laughter through the village.

I saw them at night lifting the grass roof on their shoulders. I ran across the fields and stood by the well, watching them place the rafters on the long bamboo posts. The men were stripped to the waist and their cotton trousers were boldly rolled up to their thighs. The women came with their earthen jars and hauled drinking water, pausing in the clear moonlight to watch the men with secret joy.

Then the schoolhouse was finished. I heard the bell ring joyfully in the village. I ran to the window and saw boys and girls going to school. I saw Father on our *carabao*, riding off toward our house. I took my straw hat off the wall and rushed to the gate.

Father bent down and reached for my hands. I sat behind him on the bare back of the animal and we drove crazily to the schoolhouse. We kicked the animal with our heels. The children shouted and slapped their bellies. When we reached the school yard the *carabao* stopped without warning. Father fell on the ground and rolled into the well, screaming aloud when he touched the water. I grabbed the animal's tail and hung on it till it rolled on its back in the dust.

I rushed to the well and lowered the wooden bucket. I tied the rope to the post and shouted for help. Father climbed slowly up the rope to the mouth of the well. The bigger boys came down and helped me pull Father out. He stood in the sun and shook the water off his body. He told me to go into the schoolhouse with the other children.

We waited for the teacher to come. Father followed me inside and sat on a bench at my back. When the teacher arrived we stood as one person and waited for him to be seated. Father came to my bench and sat quietly for a long time. The teacher started talking in our dialect, but he talked so fast we could hardly understand him.

When he had distributed some little Spanish books, Father got up and asked what language we would learn. The teacher told us that it was Spanish. Father asked him if he knew English. He said he knew only Spanish and our dialect. Father took my hand and we went out of the schoolhouse. We rode the *carabao* back to our house.

Father was disappointed. He had been carrying my brother's letter for almost three years now. It was still unread. The suspense was hurting him and me, too. He wanted me to learn English so that I would be able to read it to him. It was the only letter he had received in all the years that I had known him, except some letters that came from the government once a year asking him to pay his taxes.

When the rains ceased, a strong typhoon came from the north and swept away the schoolhouse. The teacher gave up teaching and married a village girl. Then he took up farming and after two years his wife gave birth to twins. The men in the village never built a schoolhouse again.

I grew up suddenly and the desire to go see other places grew. It moved me like a flood. It was impossible to walk a kilometer away from our house without wanting to run away to the city. I tried to run away a few times, but whenever I reached the town, the farm always called me back. I could not leave Father because he was getting old.

Then our farm was taken away from us. I decided to go to town for a while and live with Mother and my two little sisters. I left the farm immediately, but Father remained in the village. He came to town once with a stack of wild tomatoes and bananas, but the village called him back again.

I left our town and traveled to other places. I went to Baguio in the northern part of the Philippines and worked in the market-place posing in the nude for American tourists who seemed to enjoy the shameless nudity of the natives. An American woman, who claimed that she had come from Texas, took me to Manila.

41

She was a romantic painter. When we arrived in the capital she rented a nice large house where the sun was always shining. There were no children of my age. There were men and women who never smiled. They spoke through their noses. The painter from Texas asked me to undress every morning; she worked industriously. I had never dreamed of making my living by exposing my body to a stranger. That experience made me roar with laughter for many years.

One time, while I was still at the woman's house, I remembered the wide ditch near our house in the village where young girls used to take a bath in the nude. A cousin of mine stole the girls' clothes and then screamed behind some bushes. The girls ran at random with their hands between their legs. I thought of this incident when I felt shy, hiding my body with my hands from the woman painter. When I had saved a little money I took a boat for America.

I forgot my village for a while. When I went to a hospital and lay in bed for two years, I started to read books with great hunger. My reading was started by a nurse who thought I had come from China. I lied to her without thinking of it, but I made a good lie. I had had no opportunity to learn when I was outside in the world but the security and warmth of the hospital had given it to me. I languished in bed for two years with great pleasure. I was no longer afraid to live in a strange world and among strange peoples.

Then at the end of the first year, I remembered the letter of my brother Berto. I crept out of bed and went to the bathroom. I wrote a letter to Father asking him to send the letter to me for translation. I wanted to translate it, so that it would be easy for him to find a man in our village to read it to him.

The letter arrived in America six months later. I translated it into our dialect and sent it back with the original. I was now better. The doctors told me that I could go out of the hospital. I used to stand by the window for hours asking myself why I had forgotten to laugh in America. I was afraid to go out into the world. I had been confined too long. I had forgotten what it was like on the outside.

I had been brought to the convalescent ward when the Civil War in Spain started some three years before. Now, after the peasants' and workers' government was crushed, I was physically ready to go out into the world and start a new life. There was some indignation against fascism in all the civilized lands. To most of us, however, it was the end of a great cause.

I stood at the gate of the hospital, hesitating. Finally, I closed my eyes and walked into the city. I wandered in Los Angeles for some time looking for my brothers. They had been separated from me since childhood. We had, separately and together, a bitter fight for existence. I had heard that my brother Nicasio was in Santa Barbara, where he was attending college. Berto, who never stayed in one place for more than three months at a time, was rumored to be in Bakersfield waiting for the grape season.

I packed my suitcase and took a bus to Santa Barbara. I did not find my brother there. I went to Bakersfield and wandered in the streets asking for my other brother. I went to Chinatown and stood in line for the free chop suey that was served in the gambling houses to the loafers and gamblers. I could not find my brother in either town. I went to the vineyards looking for him. I was convinced that he was not in that valley. I took a bus for Seattle.

The hiring halls were full of men waiting to be shipped to the canneries in Alaska. I went to the dance halls and poolrooms. But I could not find my brothers. I took the last boat to Alaska and worked there for three months. I wanted to save my money so that I could have something to spend when I returned to the mainland.

When I came back to the United States, I took a bus to Portland. Beyond Tacoma, near the district where Indians used to force the hop pickers into marriage, I looked out the window and saw my brother Berto in a beer tavern. I knew it was my brother although I had not seen him for many years. There was something in the way he had turned his head toward the bus that made me think I was right. I stopped at the next town and took another bus back to Tacoma. But he was already gone.

I took another bus and went to California. I stopped in Delano. The grape season was in full swing. There were many workers in town. I stood in the poolrooms and watched the players. I went to a beer place and sat in a booth. I ordered several bottles and pondered over my life in America.

Toward midnight a man in a big overcoat came in and sat beside me. I asked him to drink beer with me without looking at his face. We started drinking together and then, suddenly, I saw a familiar face in the dirty mirror on the wall. I almost screamed. He was my brother Nicasio—but he had grown old and emaciated. We went outside and walked to my hotel.

The landlady met me with a letter from the Philippines. In my room I found that my letter to Father, when I was in the hospital, and the translation of my brother Berto's letter to him had been returned to me. It was the strangest thing that ever happened to me. I had never lived in Delano before. I had never given my forwarding address to anybody. The letter was addressed to me at a hotel I had never seen before.

It was now ten years since my brother Berto had written the letter to Father. It was eighteen years since he had run away from home. I stood in the center of my room and opened it. The note attached to it said that Father had died some years before. It was signed by the postmaster of my town.

I bent down and read the letter—the letter that had driven me away from my village and had sent me half way around the world—read it the very day a letter came from the government telling me that my brother Berto was already serving in the Navy—and the same day that my brother Nicasio was waiting to be inducted into the Army. I held the letter in my hand and, suddenly, I started to laugh—choking with tears at the mystery and wonder of it all.

"Dear Father (my brother wrote): America is a great country. Tall buildings. Wide good land. The people walking. But I feel sad. I am writing you this hour of my sentimental. Your son.— Berto."

As Long as the Grass Shall Grow

In the middle of that year when we were picking peas on the hillside, I noticed the school children playing with their teacher in the sun. It was my first time to see her, a young woman of about twenty-five, with brown hair and a white dress spotted with blue. The blue sky seemed to absorb the white color of her dress, but from where I stood she appeared all clothed in light blue. The blueness of the sea at the back of the schoolhouse also enhanced the blue dots of her dress. But my eyes were familiar with the bright colors of the hillside, the yellowing leaves of the peas, the sprouting green blades of the summer grass, the royal white gowns of the edelweiss, and the tall gray mountains in the distance, and the silent blue sea below the clear sky.

I had arrived in America, the new land, three months before and had come to this farming town to join friends who had years ago left the Philippines. I had come in time to pick the summer peas. I had been working for over a month now with a crew of young Filipino immigrants who followed the crops and the seasons. At night when our work was done and we had all eaten and scrubbed the dirt off our bodies, I joined them in dress suit and went to town to shoot pool at a familiar place. I observed that the older men went to the back of the poolroom and played cards all night long. In the morning they went to the field sleepily and talked about their losses and winnings all day. They seemed a bunch of contented workers, but they were actually restless and [had] no plans for the future.

Then I saw the children. They reminded me of a vanished time. I used to stop at my work and watch them singing and running and screaming in the sun. One dark-haired boy in particular, about eight, brought back acute memories of a childhood friend who had died a violent death when I was ten. We had gone to the fields across the river that afternoon to fly our kites because it was summertime and the breeze was just strong enough to carry our playthings to high altitudes. Suddenly, in the midst of our sport, a ferocious carabao broke loose from its peg and came plunging wildly after us, trapping my friend and goring him to death. That night when I went to see him, and realized that he was truly dead, I ran out of the house and hid in the back yard where the moonlight was like a silver column in the guava trees. I stood sobbing under a guava, smelling the sweetness of papaya blossoms in the air. Then suddenly mynas burst into a glorious song. I stopped crying and listened to them. Gradually I became vaguely comforted and could accept the fact that my friend would not come back to life again. I gathered an armful of papaya blossoms and went back into the house and spread them over the coffin. I returned to the guava grove and listened to the mynas sing.

So this dark-haired boy in a land far away, many years afterward, stirred a curiosity for the unknown in me that had been dimmed by time. I walked to the schoolhouse one morning and stood by the fence. The children ran to me as if they knew me. I can't remember now my exact feeling when they reached out their little hands to me. But I know that I suddenly started gathering the red and yellow poppies growing abundantly on the hillside. Then the teacher came out on the porch and called the children back to their classes.

I returned to my work, watching the schoolhouse. In the early afternoon when the children had gone home, I saw the teacher walking toward the hill. She came to me.

"Were you the boy who was at the schoolhouse this morning?" she asked.

"Yes, ma'am," I said.

"How old are you?"

I told her. She looked for a moment toward my companions, who had all stopped working to listen to her.

"You are too young to be working," she said finally. "How far have you gone in school?"

I was ashamed to admit it, but I said: "Third grade, ma'am."

"Would you like to do some reading under me?"

"I'd love to, ma'am," I said softly. I looked at my companions from the corner of my eyes, because they would ridicule me if they knew that I wanted some education. I never saw any reading material at our bunkhouse except the semi-nude pictures of women in movie magazines. "I'd love to study some, ma'am," I said, "but I can read only a few words."

"Well, I'll teach you," she said. "What time do you go home?"

"Six o'clock, ma'am," I said.

She said, "I'll be at your bunkhouse at eight. That will give you two hours for dinner and a bath. Tell your friends to be ready, too."

"Yes, ma'am," I said. "I will tell them. Some of them went to

46

high school in the Islands, but most of us stopped in the primary grades."

"I'll teach those who are willing," she said. "So be ready at eight sharp."

I watched her walk slowly down the hill. When she reached the highway at the foot of the hill, I waved my hand at her. She waved back and walked on. She drove away in her car, and when she was gone, I went on working quietly. But my companions taunted me. Some of them even implied certain dark things that made me stop picking peas and look at them with a challenge in my eyes. When they finally stopped shouting at me, I resumed my work thinking of some books I would like to read.

The teacher came at the appointed time. She had put on a pair of corduroy pants and an unpressed blue shirt. It was my first time to see a woman dressed like a man. I stole glances at her every time she turned her face away. She brought a story about ancient times which she read slowly to me. But I was disappointed because my companions did not want to study with me. I noticed that five stayed home and played poker; the others went to town to shoot pool. There was one in the kitchen who kept playing his guitar, stopping only now and then to listen to what we were reading. About ten o'clock in the evening the teacher closed the book and prepared to go. I took her to the door and looked outside where the moon was shining brightly. The grass on the hill was beautiful, and the calm sea farther away was like a polished mirror, and the tall mountains [on] the horizon were like castles.

"Shall I walk you to the road, ma'am?" I asked.

"Thank you," she said, shaking her head. "I love to walk in the moonlight."

When she was at the gate, I ran after her.

"What is your name, ma'am?" I asked.

"Helen O'Reilly," she said. "Goodnight."

I watched her walk away. She stopped under the tall eucalyptus trees on the highway and looked around in the wide silence. After a while she lighted a cigarette and climbed into her car.

Miss O'Reilly came to our bunkhouse every evening after that night. She read stories of long ago, and pages from the history of many nations. My companions slowly joined our course, and in two weeks only three of the whole crew stayed away. She took great interest in her work. After a while she started talking about herself

47

and the town where she had come from and about her people. She was born in a little town somewhere in the Northwest. She had come from a poor family and supported herself through college. Before she graduated the depression came. When she was offered a teaching job in a rural community in California, she accepted it thinking that she could go on with her studies when she had saved enough money.

Miss O'Reilly was a good teacher. We started giving her peas and flowers that we picked on the hillside when we were working. Once we thought of buying her a dress, but one of the elder men said that it was improper. So we put the money in a large envelope and gave it to her when she came one evening. She did not want to accept it, but we said that it was a token of our gratitude. She took it then, and when she came again she showed us a gabardine suit that she had bought with it.

We were all very happy then. On the hillside, when we were picking peas, we sometimes stopped and considered the possibility of giving her a party at our bunkhouse. But one evening she came to tell us that some organization in town had questioned her coming out to our bunkhouse. She told us to go to the school-house when our work was done and study there like regular pupils.

I could not understand why any organization would forbid her to work where she pleased. I was too newly arrived from the Islands, too sheltered within my group of fellow Filipinos to have learned the taboos of the mainland, to have seen the American doors shut against us. But I went to the schoolhouse every night with my companions and started writing short sentences on the blackboard. I stood there and looked out of the window. I saw the silent sea and the wide clear sky. Suddenly I wrote a poem about what I saw outside in the night. Miss O'Reilly started laughing because my lines were all wrong and many of the words were misspelled and incorrectly used.

"Now, now," Miss O'Reilly said behind my back, "it's too soon for you to write poetry. We will come to that later."
I blushed.
"What made you do it?" she asked.
"I don't know, Miss O'Reilly," I said.
"Did you ever read poetry before?"
"No, Miss O'Reilly," I said. "I didn't even know it was poetry."

She looked at me with some doubt. Then she went to her table and started reading from the Bible. It was the Song of Solomon. I liked the rich language, the beautiful imagery, and the depth of the old man's passion for the girl and the vineyard.

"This is the best poetry in the world," Miss O'Reilly said when she finished the chapter. "I would like you to remember it. There was a time when men loved deeply and were not afraid to love."

I was touched by the songs. I thought of the pea vines on the hillside and the silent blue sea not far away. And I said to myself: *Some day I will come back in memory to this place and time and write about you, Miss O'Reilly. How gratifying it will be to come back to you with a book in my hands about all that we are feeling here tonight!*

Miss O'Reilly shoved the Bible into my pocket that night. I read it over and over. I read all the school books also. I was beginning to think that when I could save enough money I would live in another town and go to school. We still had the peas to pick and after that the tomatoes on the other side of the hill.

Then Miss O'Reilly told us she was forbidden by the school board to use the building at night. The directive was for us, of course. Miss O'Reilly did not tell us that, but some of my companions knew what it was all about. When she invited us to go to her boarding house, only a few of us went.

"Come one by one in the dark," she advised us. "And go up the steps very quietly."

"All right, Miss O'Reilly," I said.

So we went to her room at night where we read softly. She told us that there was a sick old woman in the house. One night a man knocked on the door and asked Miss O'Reilly to step out in the hallway for a moment. When Miss O'Reilly came back to the room, I saw that she was perturbed. She looked at us in a maternal way and then toward the hallway with a forgiving look. We resumed our reading, and at our departure Miss O'Reilly told us not to mind anything.

I went again the following night. But I was alone. My companions dropped out. Miss O'Reilly seemed about to tell me something, but she let it drop. I forgot about her uneasiness as we read to each other, but when I left and she accompanied me to the door, she turned suddenly and ran to her room. I thought she had forgotten to give me something, but when her lights went out I went on my way.

I had gone two blocks away when four men approached me in the dark street. Two of them grabbed me and pushed me into a car. Then they drove me for several blocks, turned to a field of carrots, and stopped under a high water tank. They got out of the car then and started beating me.

I tried to defend myself, but they were too many. When I had a chance, however, I started to run away, but a man jumped into the car and drove after me. I fell down when the car struck me. They all came and started beating me again. I could not fight back any more. I rolled on my stomach when they kicked me. Once, when I was losing consciousness, I felt the hard heel of a shoe on the back of my head. Then everything was in darkness.

When I regained my senses, it was past midnight. The sky was as clear as day. I did not know where I was for a moment. I saw the full moon hanging languidly for a moment. I opened my swollen eyes a little and the golden lights of several stars appeared in the depth of the sky. Slowly I realized what had happened. And then, when I understood it all, tears rolled down my cheeks and fell on the cool carrot leaves underneath my head.

It was the final warning. When I reached our bunkhouse, my companions were crowded into the kitchen reading a roughly written message that had been thrown into the place that night. The men who had beaten me had driven to the bunkhouse when they were through with me.

One of the older men, who had known darker times in this land, took me by the arm and secreted me in the outer house, saying, "I could have told you these things before, but I saw that you were truly interested in educating yourself. I admired your courage and ambition. May I shake your hand?"
I said, taking his, "Thank you."
"Some men are good, but others are bad," he said again. "But all evil is not confined in one race of people, not all goodness in another. There is evil in every race, but there is also goodness in every other. And yet all the goodness belongs to the whole human race."

Then I knew why Miss O'Reilly had come to our bunkhouse and taught us. But I did not go to her boarding house for a week. I was afraid. When my bruises were well enough, I went to town, but Miss O'Reilly's room was closed and dark. I thought she had gone to a movie; I waited almost all night.

But she did not appear that night. Nor any other night. Then I knew that she had moved to another house, because during the day I saw her in the school yard. Sometimes she stopped and waved her hand toward us. I waved mine, too. And that went on for days. And then she disappeared.

I often wondered what had happened to her. Another teacher took her place. But the new teacher did not even notice us. So at night and on our days off we went to town in separate groups looking for our teacher. But we did not find her. We finished picking the peas and we moved on to the other side of the hill to harvest the tomatoes. Now and then we stopped to look toward the schoolhouse, but Miss O'Reilly did not come back. Then one day in June the schoolhouse closed its door and we watched the children slowly walk home. It was the end of another school year, but it was only the beginning of my first year in the new land.

One day, toward the end of the tomato season, Miss O'Reilly appeared. She looked a little thinner. I noticed a scar on her left wrist.

"I was in the hospital for a while," she greeted us. "I have been ill."

"You should have let us know," I said. "We would have sent you some flowers from the hill."

"That is nice of you," she said to me. "But now I am leaving. Going to the big city."

"Will you come back some day, Miss O'Reilly?" I asked.

"I hope so," she said. "But when you come to the big city, try to look for me. I think I'll be there for a long time."

"Are you going to teach in another school?"

"I don't know," she said. "But I will try to find an assignment. Yes, there must be a vacancy somewhere." And then, kindly, she put her hand on my head, saying, "I will go on teaching people like you to understand things as long as the grass shall grow."

It was like a song. I did not know then what she meant, but the words followed me down the years. That night we gave Miss O'Reilly a party at our bunkhouse. We roasted a pig in the open air. The men tuned up their musical instruments and played all night long. The moon was up in the sky and the sea was silent as ever. The tall mountains were still there; above them stars were shedding light to the world below. The grass on the hill was beginning to catch the morning dew. And then we took Miss O'Reilly to her car and bade her goodbye.

I wanted to cry. Tenderly she put her hand on my head.

"Remember," she said, "when you come to the big city, try to look for me. And now, goodnight to all."

And she drove away. And I never saw her again.

I went away from that town not long afterward and worked in many big cities. I would work for a long time in one place, but when the leaves of the trees started to fall, I would pack up my suitcase and go to another city. The years passed by very swiftly.

One morning I found I had been away from home for twenty years. But where was home? I saw the grass of another spring growing on the hills and in the fields. And the thought came to me that I had had Miss O'Reilly with me all the time, there in the broad fields and verdant hills of America, my home.

Be American

It was not Consorcio's fault. My cousin was an illiterate peasant from the vast plains of Luzon. When he came off the boat in San Francisco, he could neither read nor write English or Ilocano, our dialect. I met him when he arrived, and right away he had bright ideas in his head.

"Cousin, I want be American," he told me.

"Good," I said. "That is the right thing to do. But you have plenty of time. You are planning to live permanently in the United States, are you not?"

"Sure, cousin," he said. "But I want be American right away. On the boat I say, 'Consorcio stoody Engleesh right away.' Good ideeyas, eh, cousin?"

"It is," I said. "But the first thing for you to do is look for a job."

"Sure, cousin. You have joob for me?"

I did. I took him to a countryman of ours who owned a small restaurant on Kearny Street. He had not done any dishwashing in the Philippines, so he broke a few dishes before he realized that the dishes were not coconut shells that he could flagrantly throw around the place, the way he used to do in his village where coconut shells were plates and carved trunks of trees were platters and his fingers were spoons. He had never seen bread and butter before, so he lost some weight before he realized that he had to eat these basic things like the rest of us, and be an American, which was his own idea in the first place. He had never slept in a bed with a mattress before, so he had to suffer from severe cold before he realized that he had to sleep inside the bed, under the blankets, but not on top of the spread, which was what he had done during his first two weeks in America. And of course he had never worn shoes before, so he had to suffer a few blisters on both feet before he realized that he had to walk light-footed, easy, and even graceful, but not the way he used to do it in his village, which was like wrestling with a carabao or goat.

All these natural things he had to learn during his first two weeks. But he talked about his Americanization with great confidence.

"You see, cousin," he told me, "I have earned mony quick. I poot the hoot dashes in the sink, wash-wash, day come, day out, week gone—mony! Simple?"

"Fine," I said.

"You know what I done with mony?"

"No."

"I spent it all."

"On what?"

"Books. Come see my room."

I went with him to his small room at the back of the restaurant where he was working, near the washrooms. And sure enough, he had lined the four walls of his room with big books. I looked at the titles. He had a cheap edition of the classics, books on science, law and mathematics. He even had some brochures on political and governmental matters. All were books that a student or even a professor would take time to read.

I turned to my cousin. He was smiling with pride.

"Well, I hope these big books will make you an American faster," I told him.

"Sure, cousin. How long I wait?"

"Five years."

"Five years?" These was genuine surprise in his dark peasant face. "Too long. I do not wait. I make faster—one year."

"It is the law," I assured him.

"No good law. One year enough for Consorcio. He make good American citizen."

"There is nothing you can do about it."

"I change law."

"Go ahead."

"You see, cousin."

But he was puzzled. So I left him. I left San Francisco. When I saw him a year later, he was no longer washing dishes. But he still had the pardonable naivete of a peasant from the plains of Luzon.

"Where are you working now?" I asked him.

"Bakery," he said. "I make da bread. I make da donot. I make da pys."

"Where?"

"Come, cousin. I show you."

It was a small shop, a three-man affair. Consorcio was the handyboy in the place, scrubbing the floor, washing the pots and pans; and he was also the messenger. The owner was the baker, while his wife was the saleswoman. My cousin lived at the back of the building, near the washrooms. He had a cot in a corner of the dark room. But the books were gone.

"What happened to your books?" I asked him.

He looked sad. Then he said, "I sold, cousin."

"Why?"

"I cannot read. I cannot understand. Words too big and too long."

"You should begin with simple grammar books."

"Those cannot read also. What to do now, cousin?"

"You still want to be an American citizen?"

"Sure."

"Go to night school."

"Is a place like that?"

"Yes."

"No use, cousin. No money."

"The school is free," I told him. "It is for foreign-born people. For adults, so they could study American history."

"Free? I go now."

"The school opens only at night."

"I work night."

"Well, work in the daytime. Look for another job. You still want to be an American, don't you?"

"Sure. But I like boss-man. What to do?"

"Tell him the truth."

"You help me?"

I did. We went to the boss-man. I explained the matter as truthfully as I could and he understood Consorcio's problems. But he asked me to find someone to take my cousin's place, which I did too, so we shook hands around and departed in the best of humor. I helped Consorcio register at the night school, [and] looked for another job for him as janitor in an apartment building. Then I left him, wishing him the best of luck.

I worked in Alaska the next two years. When I returned to the mainland, I made it my duty to pass through San Francisco. But my cousin had left his janitor job and the night school. I could not find his new address, and it seemed that no one knew him well enough in the Filipino community.

I did not think much of his disappearance because we are a wandering people due to the nature of our lowly occupations, which take us from place to place, following the seasons. When I received a box of grapes from a friend, I knew he was working in the grape fields in either Fresno or Delano, depending on the freight mark. When I received a box of asparagus, I knew he was working in Stockton. But when it was a crate of lettuce, he was working in Santa Maria or Salinas, depending on the freight mark again. And in the summertime when I received a large barrel of salmon, I knew he was working in the salmon canneries in Alaska. There were no letters, no post cards—nothing. But these surprising boxes, crates and barrels that arrived periodically were the best letters in the world. What they contained were lovingly distributed among my city friends. Similarly, when I was [on] one of my own wanderings, which were done in cities and large towns, I sent my friend or friends unsealed envelopes bursting with the colored pictures of actresses and other beautiful women. I addressed these gifts to poolrooms and restaurants in towns where my friends had lived or worked for a season, because they were bound to go to any of these havens of the homeless wanderer. However, when another curious wanderer opened the envelopes and pilfered the pictures, it was not a crime. The enjoyment which was originally intended for my friends was his and his friends'. That is the law of the nomad: finders keepers.

But Consorcio had not yet learned the unwritten law of the nomad. I did not expect him to send me boxes, crates, and barrels from faraway Alaska. So I did not know where I could locate him.

I wandered in and out of Los Angeles the next two years. At the beginning of the third year, when I was talking to the sleeping birds in Pershing Square, I felt a light hand on my shoulders. I was not usually curious about hands, but it was well after midnight and the cops were wandering in and out of the place. So I turned around—and found Consorcio.

I found a new Consorcio. He had aged and the peasant naivete was gone from his face. In his eyes was now a hidden fear. His hands danced and flew when he was talking, and even when he was not talking, as though he were slapping the wind with both hands or clapping with one hand. Have you ever heard the noise of one hand clapping?

That was Consorcio, after five years in America. He was either slapping the wind with both hands or clapping with one hand. So I guided him out of the dark place to the lighted place, where we had coffee until the city awoke to give us another day of hope. Of course, I sat in silence for a long time because it was the year of deep silence. And Consorcio sat for a long time too, because by now he had learned to hide in the deep silence that was flung like a mourning cloak across the face of the land. When we talked, our sentences were short and punctuated by long silences. So we conversed somewhat like this:

"Been wandering everywhere."
"No job."
"Nothing anywhere."
"Where have you been all these years?"
Silence.
"No finished school?"
Silence.
"Not American citizen yet?"
"You should have told me."
"Told you what?"
"Filipinos can't become American citizens."
"Well, I could have told you. But I wanted you to learn."
"At least I speak better English now."
"This is a country of great opportunity."
Silence.
"No work?"
"No work."
"How long?"
"I have forgotten."
"Better times will come."
"You have a wonderful dream, cousin," he told me and left. He left Los Angeles for a long time. Then, two years later, I received a crate of oranges from him. The freight mark was San Jose. Now I knew he was working and had learned the unwritten law of the wanderers on this troubled earth. So as I ate his oranges, I recalled his last statement: *You have a wonderful dream, cousin...*

I had a wonderful dream. But I dreamed it for both of us, for many of us who wandered in silence.

Then the boxes and crates became more frequent. Then a barrel of salmon came from Alaska. And, finally, the letters came. My cousin Consorcio, the one-time illiterate peasant from the vast plains of Luzon, had indeed become an American without knowing it. His letters were full of wondering and pondering about many things in America. Now he realized his naivete when he had landed in San Francisco. But he realized also that he could not ask too much in a strange land. And it was this realization that liberated him from his peasant prison, his heritage, and eventually led him to a kind of work to which he dedicated his time and life until the end.

57

I was in Oregon when I received a newspaper from Consorcio, postmarked Pismo Beach. It was the first issue of his publication for agricultural workers in California. It was in English. From then on, I received all issues of his publication. For five years it existed, defending the workers and upholding the rights and liberties of all Americans, native or foreign born, so that, as he began to understand the nature of American society, he became more belligerent in his editorials and had to go to jail a few times for his ideas about freedom and peace.

Yes, indeed, Consorcio: You have become an American, a real American. And this land that we have known too well is not yet denuded by the rapacity of men. Rolling like a beautiful woman with an overflowing abundance of fecundity and murmurous with her eternal mystery, there she lies before us like a great mother. To her we always return from our prodigal wanderings and searchings for an anchorage in the sea of life; from her we always draw our sustenance and noble thoughts, to add to her glorious history.

But the war came. And war ended Consorcio's newspaper work and his crusade for a better America. And it ended his life also. When he was brought back from overseas, he knew he would not last long. But he talked the way he had written his editorials, measured sentences that rang like music, great poetry, and soft, soft. He would not shed a tear; but his heart must have been crying, seeing eternal darkness coming toward him, deep, deep in the night of perpetual sleep. Yes, he would not shed a tear; but he must have been crying, seeing that there was so much to do with so little time left. There was in his voice a kindness for me—unhappy, perhaps, that he could not impart what he had learned from his wanderings on this earth; unhappy, also, because he knew that it would take all the people to unmake the unhappiness which had caught up with us. And now, fifteen years after his arrival in San Francisco, he was dying.

And he died. But at least he received his most cherished dream: American citizenship. He did realize later that he had become an American before he received his papers, when he began to think and write lovingly about *our* America. He gave up many things, and finally his own life, to realize his dream.

But Consorcio is not truly dead. He lives again in my undying love for the American earth. And soon, when I see the last winter coming to the last leaf, I will be warm with the thought that another wanderer shall inherit the wonderful dream which my cousin and I had dreamed and tried to realize in America.

I Would Remember

I first saw death when I was a small boy in the little village where I was born. It was a cool summer night and the sky was as clear as day and the ripening rice fields were golden in the moonlight. I remember that I was looking out the window and listening to the sweet mating calls of wild birds in the tall trees nearby when I heard my mother scream from the dark corner of the room where she had been lying for several days because she was big with child. I ran to her to see what was going on, but my grandmother darted from somewhere in the faint candlelight and held me close to the warm folds of her cotton skirt.

My mother was writhing and kicking frantically at the old woman who was attending her, but when the child was finally delivered and cleaned I saw that my mother was frothing at the mouth and slowly becoming still. She opened her eyes and tried to look for me in the semi-darkness, as though she had something important to tell me. Then she closed her eyes and lay very still.

My grandmother took me to the field at the back of our house and we sat silently under the bending stalks of rice for hours and once, when I looked up to push away the heavy grain that was tickling my neck, I saw the fleeting shadow of a small bird across the sky followed by a big bat. The small bird disappeared in the periphery of moonlight and darkness, shrieking fiercely when the bat caught up with it somewhere there beyond the range of my vision. Then I thought of my mother who had just died and my little brother who was born to take her place, but my thoughts of him created a terror inside me and when my grandmother urged me to go back to the house I burst into tears and clutched desperately at two huge stalks of rice so that she could not pull me away. My father came to the field then and carried me gently in his arms, and I clung tightly to him as though he alone could assuage my grief and protect me from all the world.

I could not understand why my mother had to die. I could not understand why my brother had to live. I was fearful of the motives of the living and the meaning of their presence on the earth. And I felt that my little brother, because he had brought upon my life a terrorizing grief, would be a stranger to me forever and ever. It was my first encounter with death; so great was its impress on my thinking that for years I could not forget my mother's pitiful cries as she lay dying.

My second encounter with death happened when I was ten year old. My father and I were plowing in the month of May. It was raining hard that day and our only working carabao was tired and balked at moving. This animal and I grew up together like brothers; he was my constant companion in the fields and on the hillsides at the edge of our village when the rice was growing.

My father, who was a kind and gentle man, started beating him with sudden fury. I remember that there was a frightening thunderclap somewhere in the world, and I looked up suddenly toward the eastern sky and saw a wide arc of vanishing rainbow. It was then that my father started beating our carabao mercilessly. The animal jumped from the mud and ran furiously across the field, leaving the wooden plow stuck into the trunk of a large dead tree. My father unsheathed his sharp bolo and raced after him, the thin blade of the steel weapon gleaming in the slanting rain. At the edge of a deep pit where we burned felled trees and huge roots, the carabao stopped and looked back; but sensing the anger of my father, he plunged headlong into the pit. I could not move for a moment, then I started running madly toward the pit.

My father climbed down the hole and looked at the carabao with tears in his eyes. I do not know if they were tears of sadness or of repressed fury. But when I had climbed down after him, I saw big beads of sweat rolling down his forehead, mingling with his tears and soaking his already wet ragged farmer's clothes. The carabao had broken all his legs and he was trembling and twisting in the bottom of the pit. When my father raised the bolo in his hands to strike at the animal, I turned away and pressed my face in the soft embankment. Then I heard his hacking at the animal, grunting and cursing in the heavy rain.

When I looked again the animal's head was completely severed from the body, and warm blood was flowing from the trunk and making a red pool under our feet. I wanted to strike my father, but instead, fearing and loving him, I climbed out of the pit quickly and ran through the blinding rain to our house.

Twice now I had witnessed violent deaths. I came across death again some years afterward on a boat when, on my way to America, I befriended a fellow passenger of my age named Marco.

He was an uneducated peasant boy from the northern part of our island who wanted to earn a little money in the new land and return to his village. It seemed there was a girl waiting for him when he came back, and although she was also poor and uneducated, Marco found happiness in her small brown face and simple ways. He showed me a faded picture of her and ten dollars he had saved up to have it enlarged when we arrived in the new land.

Marco had a way of throwing back his head and laughing loudly, the way peasants do in that part of the island. But he was quick and sensitive; anger would suddenly appear in his dark face, then fear, and then laughter again; and sometimes all these emotions would simultaneously appear in his eyes, his mouth, his whole face. Yet he was sincere and honest in whatever he did or said to me.

I got seasick the moment we left Manila, and Marco started hiding oranges and apples in his suitcase for me. Fruits were the only things I could eat, so in the dead of night when the other passengers were stirring in their bunks and peering through the dark to see what was going on, I sat up. Suddenly there was a scream and someone shouted for the light. I ran to the corner and clicked the switch and when the room was flooded with light, I saw Marco lying on the floor and bleeding from several knife wounds on his body. I knelt beside him, but for a moment only, because he held my hands tightly and died. I looked at the people around me and then asked them to help me carry the body to a more comfortable place. When the steward came down to make an inventory of Marco's suitcase, the ten dollars was gone. We shipped back the suitcase, but I kept the picture of the girl.

I arrived in America when thousands of people were waiting in line for a piece of bread. I kept on moving from town to town, from one filthy job to another, and then many years were gone. I even lost the girl's picture and for a while forgot Marco and my village.

I met Crispin in Seattle in the coldest winter of my life. He had just arrived in the city from somewhere in the east and he had no place to stay. I took him to my room and for days we slept together, eating what we could buy with the few cents that we begged in gambling houses from night to night. Crispin had drifted most of his life and he could tell me about other cities. He was very gentle and there was something luminous about him, like the strange light that flashes in my mind when I sometimes think of the hills of home. He had been educated and he recited poetry with a sad voice that made me cry. He always spoke of goodness and beauty in the world.

It was a new experience and the years of loneliness and fear were shadowed by the grace of his hands and the deep melancholy of his eyes. But the gambling houses were closed toward the end of that winter and we could not beg anymore from the gamblers because they were also starving. Crispin and I used to walk in the snow for hours looking for nothing, waiting for the cold night to fall, hoping for the warm sun to come out of the dark sky. And then one night when we had not eaten for five days, I got out of bed and ate several pages of an old newspaper by soaking them in a can of water from the faucet in our room. Choking tears came out of my eyes, but the deep pain in my head burst wide open and blood came out of my nose. I finally went to sleep from utter exhaustion, but when I woke up again, Crispin was dead.

Yes, it was true. He was dead. He had not even contemplated death. Men like Crispin who had poetry in their soul come silently into the world and live quietly down the years, and yet when they are gone no moon in the sky is lucid enough to compare with the light they shed when they are among the living.

After nearly a decade of wandering and rootlessness, I lost another good friend who had guided me in times of helplessness. I was in California in a small agricultural community. I lived in a big bunkhouse of thirty farm workers with Leroy, who was a stranger to me in many ways because he was always talking about unions and unity. But he had a way of explaining the meanings of words in utter simplicity, like "work," which he translated into "power," and "power" into "security." I was drawn to him because I felt that he had lived in many places where the courage of men was tested with the cruelest weapons conceivable.

One evening I was eating with the others when several men came into our bunkhouse and grabbed Leroy from the table and dragged him outside. He had been just about to swallow a ball of rice when the men burst into the place and struck Leroy viciously on the neck with thick leather thongs. He fell on the floor and coughed up the ball of rice. Before Leroy realized what was happening to him, a big man came toward him from the darkness with a rope in his left hand and a shining shotgun in the other. He tied the rope around Leroy's neck while the other men pointed their guns at us, and when they had taken him outside, where he began screaming like a pig about to be butchered, two men stayed at the door with their aimed guns. There was some scuffling outside, then silence, and then the two men slowly withdrew with their guns, and there was a whispering sound of running feet on the newly cut grass in the yard and then the smooth purring of cars speeding away toward the highway and then there was silence again.

We rushed outside all at once, stumbling against each other. And there hanging on a tall eucalyptus tree, naked and shining in the pale light of the April moon, Leroy was swinging like a toy balloon. We cut him down and put him on the grass, but he died the moment we reached him. His genitals were cut and there was a deep knife wound in his chest. His left eye was gone and his tongue was sliced into tiny shreds. There was a wide gash across his belly and his entrails plopped out and spread on the cool grass.

That is how they killed Leroy. When I saw his cruelly tortured body, I thought of my father and the decapitated carabao and the warm blood flowing under our bare feet. And I knew that all my life I would remember Leroy and all the things he taught me about living.

Homecoming

Already, through the coming darkness, he could see landmarks of familiar places. He stirred as he looked out of the window, remembering scenes of childhood. Houses flew by him; the sudden hum of human activity reached his ears. He was nearing home.

He kept his eyes upon the narrowing landscape. When the bus drove into town and stopped under the big arbor tree that was the station, he rushed from his seat and jumped onto the ground, filled with joy and wonder and mystery.

The station was deserted. He found the old road that ran toward his father's house. He walked in the darkness, between two long rows of houses. A little dog shot out from a house and barked at him. He looked at it with a friendly smile. He wanted to stop and pick up a handful of the earth of home, but thoughts of his people loomed large in his mind. Every step brought vivid recollections of his family. He was bursting with excitement, not knowing what to say. He walked on in the thickening darkness.

He had gone to America twelve years before, when he was fifteen. And now that he was back, walking on the dirt road that he had known so well, he felt like a boy of fifteen again. Yes, he was barely fifteen when he left home. He began to remember how one evening he ran like mad on this road with some roots that the herbalist needed for his mother, who was sick in bed with a mysterious disease. He had cried then, hugging the roots close to him. He knew that the fate of his mother was in his hands; he knew that they were waiting for him.... A mist came to his eyes. Reliving this tragic moment of childhood, he began to weaken with sudden tenderness for his mother. He walked faster, remembering...

Then he came to the gate of his father's house. For some moments he stood before the house, his heart pounding painfully. And now he knew. This was what he had come for—a little grass house near the mountains, away from the riot and madness of cities. He had left the civilization of America for this tiny house, and now that he was here, alone, he felt weak inside. He was uncertain.

For a moment he was afraid of what the house would say; he was afraid of what the house would ask him. The journey homeward had been more than eight thousand miles of land and water, but now that he was actually standing before the house, it seemed as if he had come from a place only a few miles away.

He surveyed the house in the dark, lost in his memories. Then he stepped forward, his feet whispering in the sand that filled the path to the house.

A faint gleam of light from the kitchen struck his face. He recalled at once that when he was young, the family always came home late in the evening; and his mother, who did all the domestic chores, served dinner around midnight. He paused a while, feeling a deep love for his mother. Then he crawled under the window, where the light shot across his face. He stood there and waited, breathless, for a moment.

But they were very quiet in the house. He could hear somebody moving toward the stove and stopping there to pour water into a jar. He found a hard object which he knew to be an empty box, and he hoisted himself on it, looking into the kitchen whence the lamp threw a beam of soft light.

Now he could see a large portion of the kitchen. He raised his heels, his eyes roving over the kitchen. Then he caught a quick glimpse of his mother, the old oil lamp in her hand. He was petrified with fear, not knowing what to do. One foot slipped from the side of the box and he hung in mid-air. He wanted to shout to her all the sorrows of his life, but a choking lump came to his throat. He looked, poised, undecided; then his mother disappeared behind a yellow curtain. His mind was a riot of conflict; he shifted from foot to foot. But action came to him at last. He jumped onto the ground and ran to the house.

He climbed up the ladder and stood by the door. His younger sister was setting the table, and his older sister, who was called Francisca, was helping his mother with the boiling pot on the stove. He watched the three women moving mechanically in the kitchen. Then he stepped forward, his leather shoes slapping against the floor. Francisca turned toward him and screamed.

"Mother!"
The mother looked swiftly from the burning stove and found the bewildered face of her son.
"It's me—Mariano—" he moved toward them, pausing at the table.
"Mother!"

They rushed to him, all of them; the moment was eternity. Marcela, the younger sister, knelt before him; she was crying wordlessly. The mother was in his arms; her white hair fell upon his shoulder. Unable to say anything sensible, he reached for Francisca and said: "You've grown..."

Francisca could not say a word; she turned away and wept. The tension of this sudden meeting was unbearable to him. And now he was sorry he had come home. He felt that he could never make them happy again; a long period of deterioration would follow this sudden first meeting. He knew it, and he revolted against it. But he also knew that he could never tell them why he had come home.

They prepared a plate for him. He was hungry and he tried to eat everything they put on his plate. They had stopped eating. They were waiting for him to say something; they were watching his every movement. There were many things to talk about, but he did not know where to begin. He was confused. The silence was so deep he could hear the wind among the trees outside. Pausing a while, a thought came to his mind. *Father:* Where was father?

He looked at Francisca. "Where is father?" he asked.

Francisca turned to her mother for guidance, [then to] Mariano's lifted face.

Finally Francisca said: "Father died a year after you left."

"Father was a very old man," Marcela added. "He died in his sleep."

Mariano wanted to believe them, but he felt that they were only trying to make it easy for him. Then he looked at his mother. For the first time he seemed to realize that she had aged enormously. Then he turned to his sisters, who had become full-grown women in his absence. A long time passed before he could say anything.

"I didn't know that," he said, looking down at his food.

"We didn't want you to know," his mother said.

"I didn't know that father died," he repeated.

"Now you know," Marcela said.

Mariano tried to swallow the hot rice in his mouth, but a big lump of pain came to his throat. He could not eat anymore. He washed his hands and reached for the cloth on the wall above the table.

"I've had enough," he said.

Marcela and Francisca washed the dishes in a tall wooden tub. The mother went to the living room and spread the thin mat on the floor. Mariano sat on the long bench, near the stove. He was waiting for them to ask questions. His eyes roved around the house, becoming intimate with the furniture. When the mother came to the kitchen, Marcela took the lamp from the wall and placed it on one end of the bench. The light rose directly toward Mariano's face.

The mother paused. "Why didn't you let us know you were coming?" she asked.

"I wanted to surprise you," he lied.

"I'm glad you are with us again."

"We're very glad," Francisca said.

"Yes," Marcela said.

Then the mother closed the window. Mariano looked at Marcela, but the light dazzled him. Now he felt angry with himself. He wanted to tell the truth, but could not. How could he make them understand that he had failed in America? How could he let them realize that he had come home because there was no other place for him in the world? At twenty-seven, he felt through with life; he knew that he had come home to die. America had crushed his spirit.

He wanted to say something, but did not know where to begin. He was confused, now that he was home. All he could say was: "I came home..."

A strong wind blew into the house, extinguishing the lamp. The house was thrown into complete darkness. He could hear Marcela moving around, fumbling for matches under the stove. In the brief instant of darkness that wrapped the house he remembered his years in the hospital. He recalled the day of his operation, when the doctor had worked on his right lung. It all came back to him. Strange: unconsciously, he placed a hand on his chest. When the match spurted in Marcela's cupped palms, Mariano drew back his hand. He watched the lamp grow brighter until the house was all lighted again.

Then he said: "I wanted to write, but there was nothing I could say."

"We knew that," the mother said.

They were silent. Mariano looked at their faces. He knew now

67

that he could never tell them what the doctor had told him before he sailed for home. Two years perhaps, the doctor had said. Yes, he had only two years left to live in the world. Two years: How much could he do in so brief a time? He began to feel weak. He looked at their faces.

Now it was his turn. Touching Marcela by the hand, he asked: "Are you all right? I mean...since father died..."

"I take laundry from students," Marcela said. "But it's barely enough. And sister here—"

Francisca rose suddenly and ran to the living room. The mother looked at Marcela. The house was electrified with fear and sadness.

"When students go back to their home towns, we have nothing."

"Is Francisca working?"

"She takes care of the Judge's children. Sister doesn't like to work in that house, but it's the only available work in town."

His heart was dying slowly.

"Mother can't go around anymore. Sister and I work to the bones. We've never known peace."

Mariano closed his eyes for a brief moment and pushed the existence of his sister out of his consciousness. The mother got up from the floor and joined Francisca in the living room. Now Mariano could hear Francisca weeping. Marcela was tougher; she looked toward the living room with hard, unsentimental eyes. Mariano was frightened, knowing what Marcela could do in a harsh world.

"Sister isn't pretty anymore," Marcela said.

Mariano was paralyzed with the sudden fear. He looked at Marcela. *Yes, she too was not pretty anymore.* But she did not care about herself; she was concerned over her sister. He looked at her cotton dress, torn at the bottom. Then he felt like smashing the whole world; he was burning with anger. He was angry against all the forces that had made his sisters ugly.

Suddenly, he knelt before Marcela. He took her hands, comprehending. Marcela's palms were rough. Her fingernails were torn like matchsticks. Mariano bit his lower lip until it bled. He knew he would say something horrible if he opened his mouth. Instead he got up and took the lamp and went to the living room.

Francisca was weeping in her mother's arms. Mariano held the lamp above them, watching Francisca's face. She turned her face away, ashamed. But Mariano saw, and now he knew. *Francisca was not pretty anymore.* He wanted to cry.

"We were hungry," Marcela said. She had followed him.

Mariano turned around suddenly and felt cold inside when he saw Marcela's cold stare in the semi-darkness. What did he not know about hunger? *Goddamn!*

"I wish I..." he stopped. Fear and anger welled up in him. Now he could understand the brevity of their answers to his questions; their swift glances that meant more than their tongues could utter. Now he could understand his mother's deadening solemnity. And Marcela's bitterness. Now it dawned on him that his mother and sisters had suffered the same terrors of poverty, the same humiliations of defeat, that he had suffered in America. He was like a man who had emerged from night into day, and found the light as blinding as the darkness.

The mother knelt on the floor, reaching for the lamp. Mariano walked back to the kitchen. He knew he could not do anything for them. He knew he could not do anything for himself. He knew he could not do anything at all. This was the life he had found in America; it was so everywhere in the world. He was confirmed now. He thought when he was in America that it could not be thus in his father's house. But it was there when he returned to find his sisters wrecked by deprivation...

Mariano stood by the window long after they had gone to bed. He stood in the darkness, waiting. The houses were silent. The entire district was quiet as a tomb. His mother was sleeping peacefully. He turned to look at his sisters in the dark. They were sleeping soundly. Then noiselessly, he walked to the bed.

Mariano leaned against the wall, thinking. After a while a child began to cry somewhere in the neighborhood. Two dogs ran across the road, chasing each other. Then a rooster began to crow, and others followed. It was almost dawn.

Now Mariano sat still in the darkness, listening. When he was sure they were deep in sleep, he got up slowly and reached for his hat on the table. He stopped at the door and looked back. He found a match in his pocket and scratched it on the panel of the door. Then he tiptoed to his mother and watched her face with tenderness. As he walked over to his sisters, the match burned out. He stood between them, trembling with indecision. Suddenly, he walked to the door and descended the ladder in a hurry.

There were a few stars in the sky. The night wind was soft. There was a touch of summer in the air. When he had passed the gate, Mariano stopped and looked back at the house. The vision of his father rose in the night. Then it seemed to him that the house of his childhood was more vivid than at any other time in that last look. He knew he would never see it again.

To My Countrymen

With a stroke of my hand, I cut the tides
That swept the destinies of men.
Now in this field of combat, where my armies
Challenged the tragic course of history:
Look, listen: cries crescenting blood,
Crimsoning our island; because I came.
Here I slapped the earth to make you a home,
Confounding fate, even the farthest star,
Where light resolved itself into your faith;
Because I came to stake a claim on the world.
And across the flaming darkness of life,
I flung a sword of defiance to give you freedom:
Here in the seven-pillared wisdom-house of truth,
Where I knelt, where I wept, where I lived
To change the course of history; because I love you.

Biography

There is no end of sadness
When winter came and sprawled over
The trees and houses, a man rose from
His sleep and kissed his wife who wept.
A child was born. Delicately the film
Of his life unfolded like a coral sea,
Where stone is a hard substance of wind
And water leading into memory like pain.
He was a young man. He looked at himself
Through a glass that was too real to image
His face, unreal before his eyes. These were vivid
To the hands; these were too real
To the hearts that bled to sustain life.
He was a man. And the sun that leaped
Into his eyes, the grass beneath his feet
That walked cobbled streets, the cities—
All were a challenge to his imagination:
But his mother decaying in a nameless grave,
And his father watching a changing world
Through iron bars, his broken childhood,
Were as real as pain locking memory.

Hymn to a Man Who Failed

Evening and the voice of a friendly river
The symmetry of stars, time flowing warm,
The perfect hour sitting on the tree-tops,
And peace, bird of shy understanding, waiting.

This is your world, this tin-can shack on the dry
River bed, this undismayed humanity drinking
Black coffee and eating stale bread, this water
Blue under the dark shadows of the proud city.

Lie down and laugh your worries away,
Or sit awhile and dream of impossible regions,
While there is no hunger, no endless waiting,
No cry for blood, no deceptions, no lies.

You are lost, lost between two uncertainties,
Between two conflicts, the mastered and the unharmed.
You are altogether alone and cold and hopeless.
The end is crouching like a tiger under your feet.

Evening and returning home, finding no peace,
No embrace of devotion, my beaten friend,
O failure who returns always to the dry river bed,
We are betrayed twice under the fabulous city.

Factory Town

The factory whistle thrilled the atmosphere
With a challenging shriek; the doors opened suddenly
And vomited black-faced men, toil-worn men:
Their feet whispered wearily upon the gravel path;
They reached the gate and looked at each other.
No words—lidless eyes moved, reaching for love.
Silence and fear made them strong, invincible, wise.
They shook their hands and tossed their heads back
In secret defiance to their fragmentary careers,
And paced the homeward road with heavy hearts.

These were the longest years of their lives;
These were the years when the whistle at four o'clock
Drove them to the yard, then they scurried
Home heavy with fatigue and hunger and love.
These were the years when the gigantic chimneys blocked
The skies with black smokes that reminded passersby
Of a serpent-like whip of life within, bleeding,
Scarred with disease and death. These were the years...

Faces behind the laced doors and curtained windows,
Did you see the young man stand by the factory gate,
His face serious and forlorn, brittled with pain,
His hands unsteady with nervousness—did you see him?
Look at the lengthening line of voiceless men waiting
By the factory gate that will never be men again.

I Want the Wide American Earth

Before the brave, before the proud builders and workers,
I say I want the wide American earth,
Its beautiful rivers and long valleys and fertile plains,
Its numberless hamlets and expanding towns and towering cities,
Its limitless frontiers, its probing intelligence,
For all the free.

Free men everywhere in my land—
This wide American earth—do not wander homeless,
And are not alone; friendship is our bread, love our air;
And we call each other comrade, each growing with the other,
Each a neighbor to the other, boundless in freedom.

I say I want the wide American earth....
I say to you defenders of freedom, builders of peace,
I say to you democratic brothers, comrades of love:
Their judges lynch us, their police hunt us;
Their armies and navies and airmen terrorize us;
Their thugs and stoolies and murderers kill us;
They take away bread from our children;
They ravage our women;
They deny life to our elders.
But I say we have the truth
On our side, we have the future with us;
We have history in our hands, our belligerent hands.
We are millions everywhere,
On seas and oceans and lands;
In air;
On water and all over this very earth.
We are millions working together.
We are building, creating, molding life.
We are shaping the shining structures of love.
We are everywhere, we are everywhere.
We are there when they sentence us to prison for telling the truth;
We are there when they conscript us to fight their wars;
We are there when they throw us in concentration camps;
We are there when they come at dawn with their guns.
We are there, we are there,
And we say to them:

"You cannot frighten us with your bombs and deaths;
You cannot drive us away from our land with your hate and disease;
You cannot starve us with your war programs and high prices;
You cannot command us with your nothing,
Because you are nothing but nothing;
You cannot put us all in your padded jails;
You cannot snatch the dawn of life from us!"

And we say to them:

"Remember, remember,
We shall no longer wear rags, eat stale bread, live in darkness;
We shall no longer kneel on our knees to your false gods;
We shall no longer beg you for a share of life.
Remember, remember,
O remember in the deepest midnight of your fear,
We shall emulate the wonder of our women,
The ringing laughter of our children,
The strength and manhood of our men
With a true and honest and powerful love!"

And we say to them:

"We are the creators of a flowering race!"

I say I want the wide American earth.
I say to you too, sharer of my delights and thoughts,
I say this deathless truth,
And more—
                    For look, watch, listen:
With a stroke of my hand I open the dawn of a new world,
Lift up the beautiful horizon of a new life;
All for you, comrade and my love.
                                        See:
The magnificent towers of our future [are] afire with truth,
And growing with the fuel of the heart of my heart,
And unfolding and unfolding, and flowering and flowering
In the bright new sun of our world;
All for you, comrade and my wife.
                                        And see:
I cry, I weep with joy,
And my tears are the tears of my people....

Before the brave, before the proud builders and workers,
I say I want the wide American earth
For all the free.
I want the wide American earth for my people.
I want my beautiful land.
I want it with my rippling strength and tenderness
Of love and light and truth
For all the free—

If You Want To Know What We Are

I

If you want to know what we are who inhabit
forest, mountain, rivershore, who harness
beast, living steel, martial music (that classless
language of the heart), who celebrate labor,
wisdom of the mind, peace of the blood;

If you want to know what we are who become
animate at the rain's metallic ring, the stone's
accumulated strength, who tremble in the wind's
blossoming (that enervates earth's potentialities),
who stir just as flowers unfold to the sun;

If you want to know what we are who grow
powerful and deathless in countless counterparts,
each part pregnant with hope, each hope supreme,
each supremacy classless, each classlessness
nourished by unlimited splendor of comradeship;

We are multitudes the world over, millions everywhere;
in violent factories, sordid tenements, crowded cities,
in skies and seas and rivers, in lands everywhere;
our numbers increase as the wide world revolves
and increases arrogance, hunger, disease and death.

We are the men and women reading books, searching
in the pages of history for the lost word, the key
to the mystery of living peace, imperishable joy;
we are factory hands field hands mill hands everywhere,
molding creating building structures, forging ahead,

Reaching for the future, nourished in the heart;
we are doctors scientists chemists discovering,
eliminating disease and hunger and antagonisms;
we are soldiers navy-men citizens guarding
the imperishable will of man to live in grandeur.

We are the living dream of dead men everywhere,
the unquenchable truth that class-memories create
to stagger the infamous world with prophecies
of unlimited happiness—a deathless humanity;
we are the living and the dead men everywhere...

78

II

If you want to know what we are, observe
the bloody club smashing heads, the bayonet
penetrating hollowed breasts, giving no mercy;
watch the bullet crashing upon armorless citizens;
look at the tear-gas choking the weakened lung.

If you want to know what we are, see the lynch
trees blossoming, the hysterical mob rioting;
remember the prisoner beaten by detectives to confess
a crime he did not commit because he was honest,
and who stood alone before a rabid jury of ten men.

And who was sentenced to hang by a judge
whose bourgeois arrogance betrayed the office
he claimed his own; name the marked man,
the violator of secrets; observe the banker,
the gangster, the mobster who kill and go free:

We are the sufferers who suffer for natural love
of man for man, who commemorate the humanities
of every man; we are the toilers who toil
to make the starved earth a place of abundance,
who transform abundance into deathless fragrance.

We are the desires of anonymous men everywhere,
who impregnate the wide earth's lustrous wealth
with a gleaming florescence; we are the new thoughts
and the new foundations, the new verdure of the mind;
we are the new hope new joy life everywhere.

We are the vision and the star, the quietus of pain;
we are the terminals of inquisition, the hiatuses
of a new crusade; we are the subterranean subways
of suffering; we are the will of dignities;
we are the living testament of a flowering race.

If you want to know what we are—
                              WE ARE REVOLUTION!

Books Consulted

For a good bibliography of Bulosan's work and related materials up to 1979, see *Amerasia Journal,* 1979, Vol. 6, No. 1, 167-72.

Because some of the important books and materials about Bulosan are still hard to locate, we suggest you check where necessary with University libraries and The Cellar Bookstore, Detroit, Michigan.

Published Works of Carlos Bulosan

The Laughter of My Father, NY, 1944. Stories of village and peasant life in the Philippines.

America Is in the Heart, Introduction by Carey McWilliams, Seattle, 1973 (first published in 1946). His major work.

Sound of Falling Light: Letters in Exile, Ed. Dolores Feria, Quezon City, Dilliman Review, 1960. Portrait of the writer's interior life. Write Wason Collection, Cornell U. Libraries.

"Writings of Carlos Bulosan," Ed. E. San Juan, Jr., *Amerasia Journal,* UCLA Asian American Studies Center, May 1979, Vol. 6, No. 1. With introduction by E. San Juan, Jr., pp. 3-29. Essays, stories, poems, selected letters on Filipinos in America.

The Power of the People, Ed. E. San Juan, Jr., Ontario, Canada 1977. Political novella. Write Prof. San Juan, Dept. of English, Univ. of Conn., Storrs, CT.

The Philippines Is in the Heart, Ed. E. San Juan, Jr., Quezon City, 1978. Folk tales, retold stories of Philippine life, edited posthumously.

Articles about Carlos Bulosan

Petronilo Bn. Daroy, "Carlos Bulosan: The Politics of Literature," *St. Louis Quarterly,* June 1968, Vol. 6, No. 2, 193-206.

E. San Juan, Jr., "Carlos Bulosan and the Imagination of the Class Struggle," *Solidarity,* September 1971, Vol. 6, No. 9, 17-25.

Historical and Literary Background

Letters in Exile, An introductory reader on the history of the Pilipinos in America, UCLA Asian American Studies Center, 1976.

Aiiieeeee!, An Anthology of Asian-American Writers, Ed. Frank Chin, Jeffrey Chan, Lawson Inada and Shawn Wong, Howard University Press, 1982 (reprint).